Grandfather
and the Moon

STÉPHANIE LAPOINTE
AND ROGÉ

Grandfather and the Moon

Translated by Shelley Tanaka

GROUNDWOOD BOOKS
HOUSE OF ANANSI PRESS
TORONTO   BERKELEY

Original Title: *Grand-père et la Lune* de Stéphanie Lapointe et Rogé
Copyright © 2015 Les Éditions XYZ Inc.
English translation copyright © 2017 by Shelley Tanaka

Published in English in Canada and the USA in 2017 by Groundwood Books

Groundwood Books / House of Anansi Press
groundwoodbooks.com

We acknowledge for their financial support of our publishing program the
Canada Council for the Arts, the Ontario Arts Council and the Government
of Canada.

We acknowledge the financial support of the Government of Canada
through the National Translation Program for Book Publishing, an initiative
of the *Roadmap for Canada's Official Languages 2013-2018: Education,
Immigration, Communities*, for our translation activities.

Canada Council   Conseil des Arts
for the Arts   du Canada

ONTARIO ARTS COUNCIL
CONSEIL DES ARTS DE L'ONTARIO
an Ontario government agency
un organisme du gouvernement de l'Ontario

With the participation of the Government of Canada   Canadä
Avec la participation du gouvernement du Canada

Library and Archives Canada Cataloguing in Publication
Lapointe, Stéphanie
[Grand-père et la Lune. English]
Grandfather and the moon / Stéphanie Lapointe ; Rogé, illustrator ;
Shelley Tanaka, translator.
Translation of: Grand-père et la Lune.
Issued in print and electronic formats.
ISBN 978-1-55498-961-4 (hardback).
—ISBN 978-1-55498-963-8 (epub).—
ISBN 978-1-77306-045-3 (kf8)
1. Graphic novels. I. Rogé, illustrator II. Tanaka, Shelley,
translator III. Title. IV. Title: Grand-père et la Lune. English
PN6733.L348G7313 2017   j741.5'971   C2016-905780-1
C2016-905781-X

The illustrations were done in mixed media.
Printed and bound in Malaysia

MIX
Paper from
responsible sources
FSC® C012700
www.fsc.org

For Marguerite,

To tell you
that maybe the best thing is not
setting foot on the moon,
but making the journey it takes
to get there.

Stéphanie

For Clara,

mon étoile,

Rogé

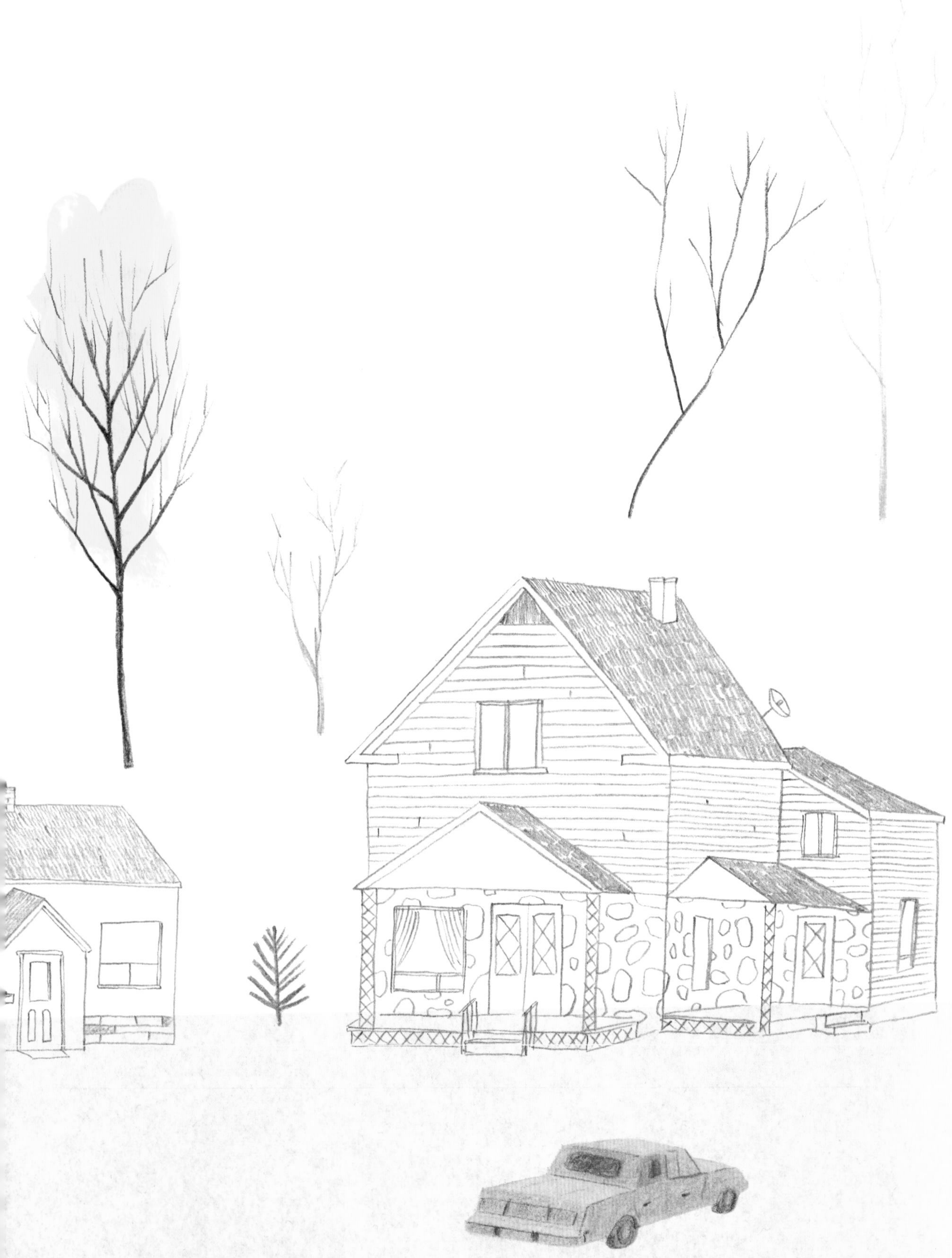

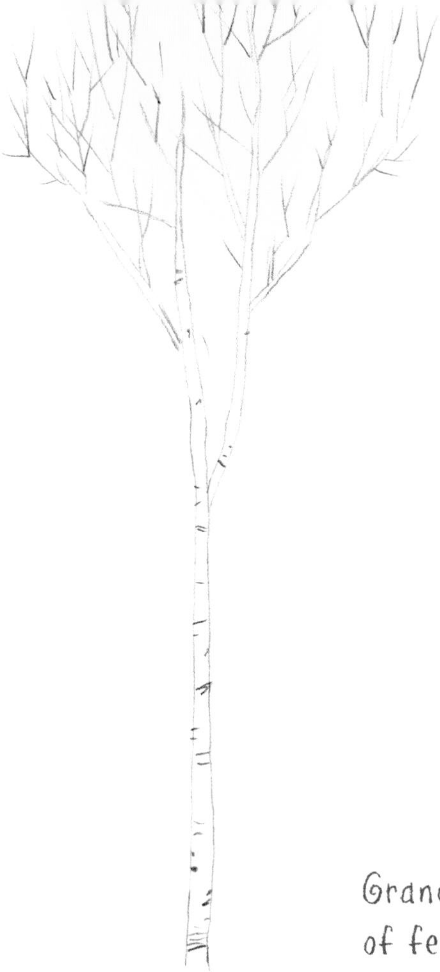

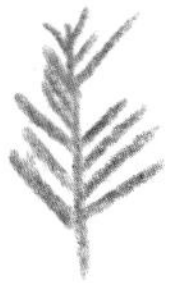

Grandfather was a man
of few words.

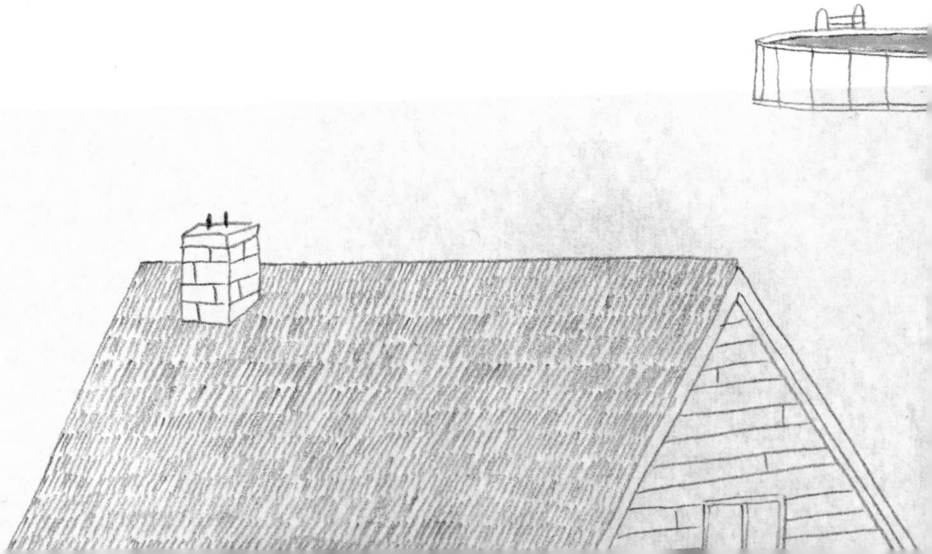

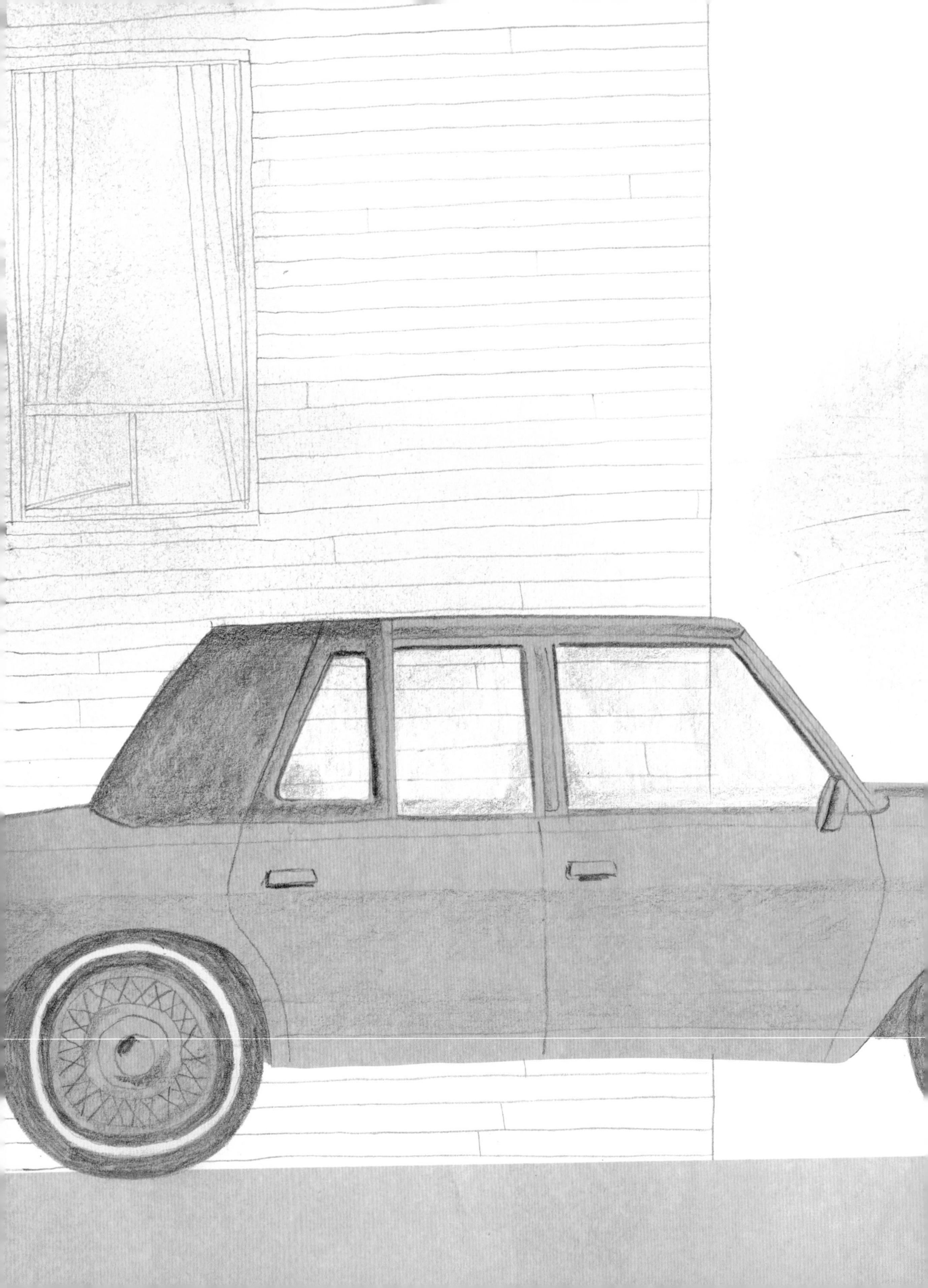

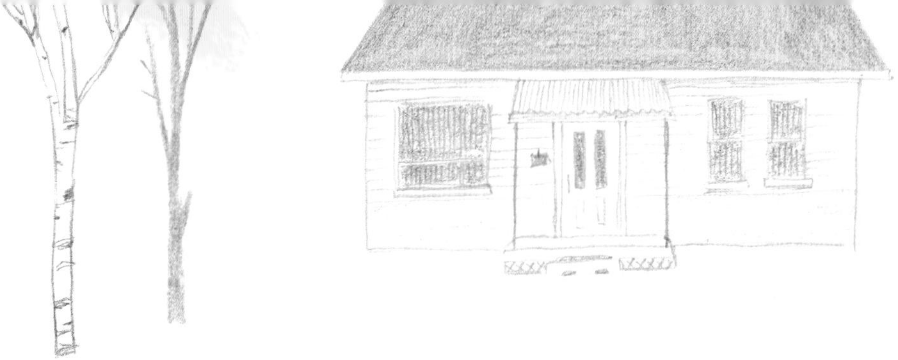

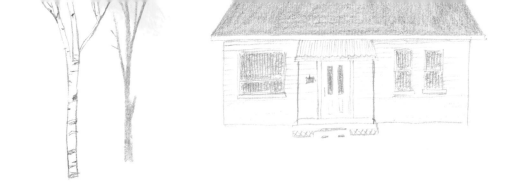

At least, that's what they said
at his funeral.

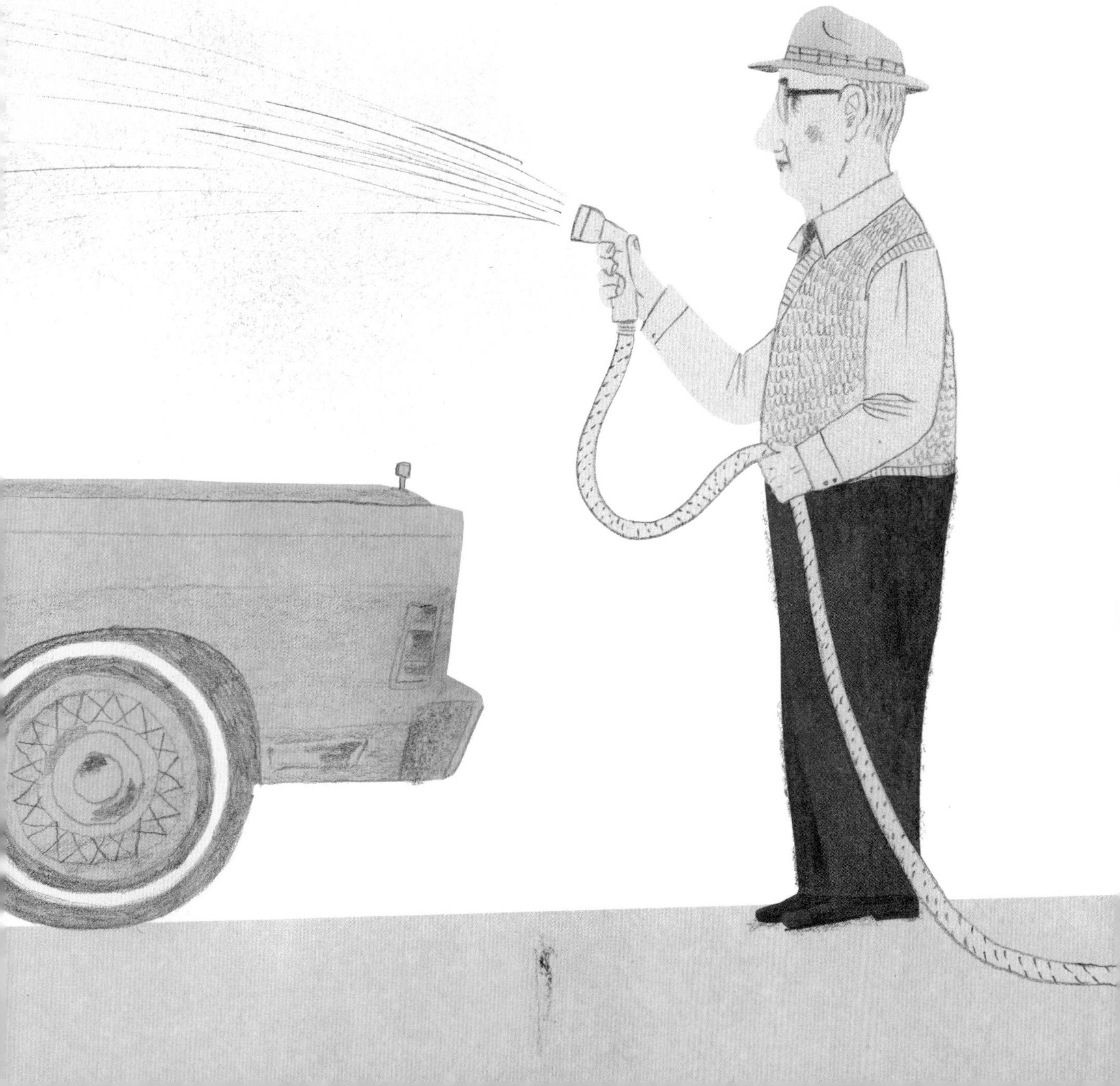

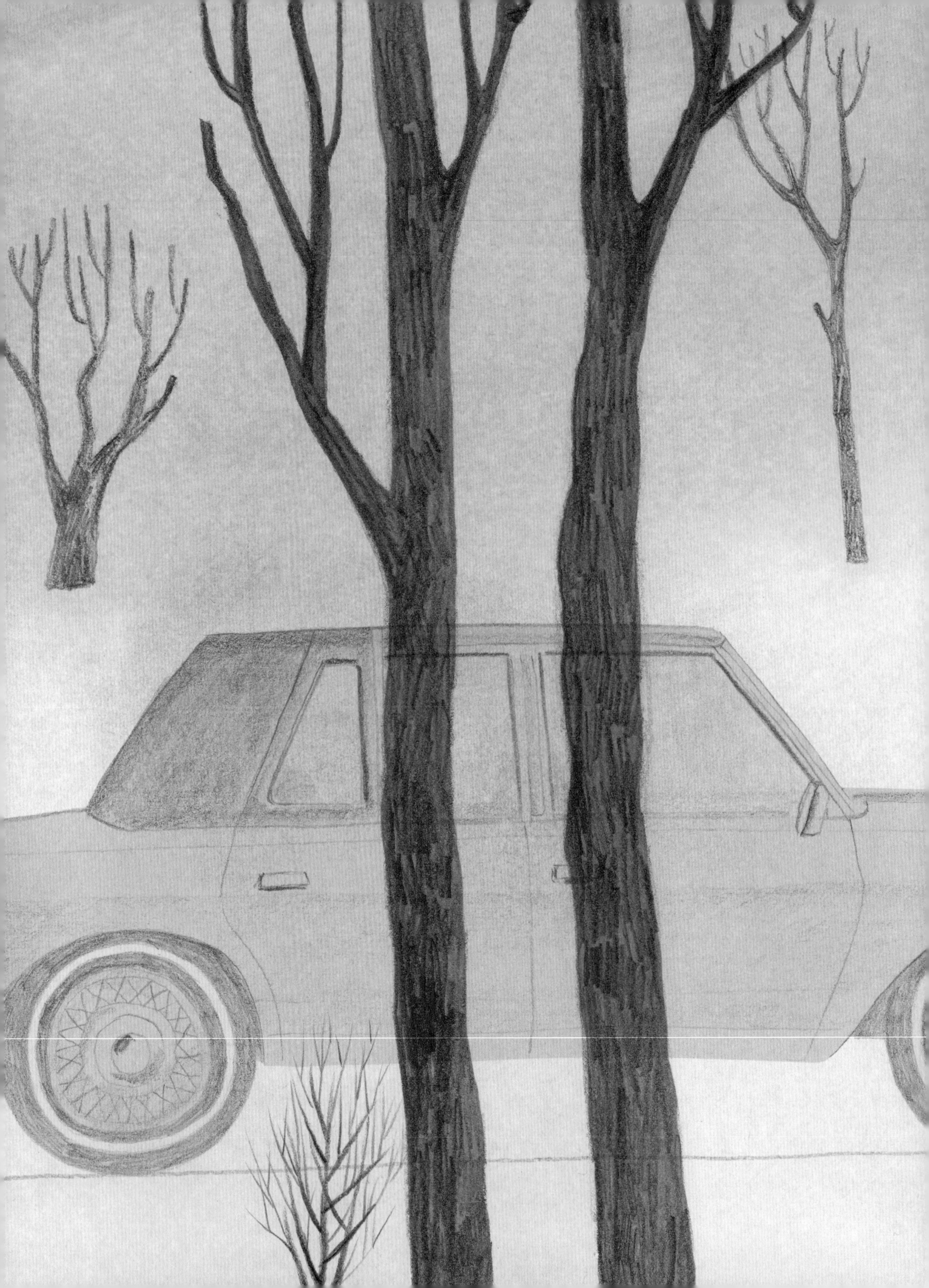

"Adrien was a man of few words."

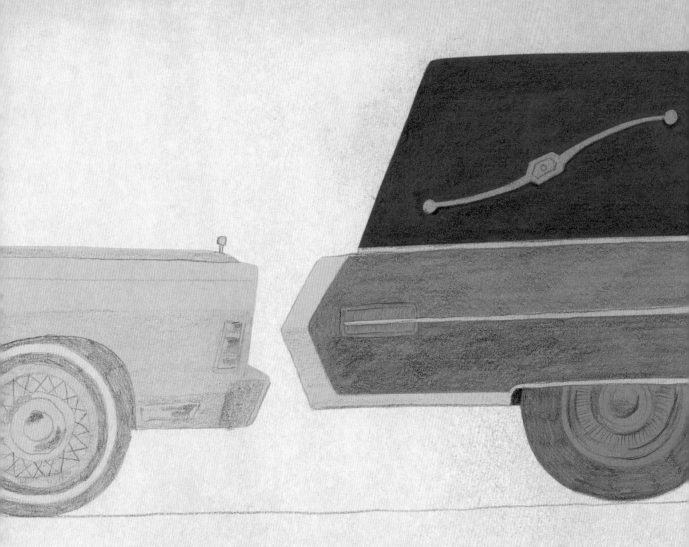

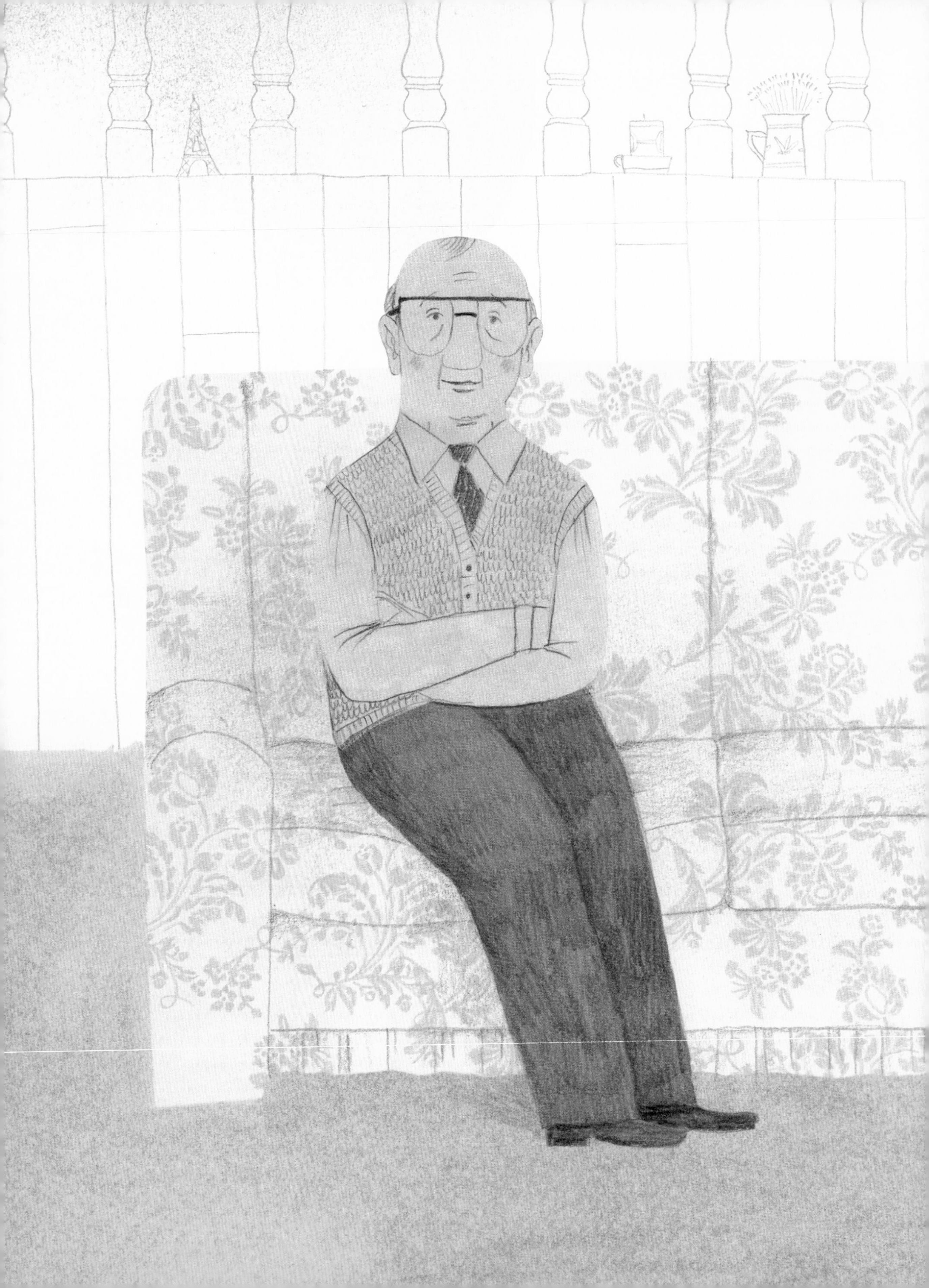

I can't say I ever said
much to him, either.
To Adrien.

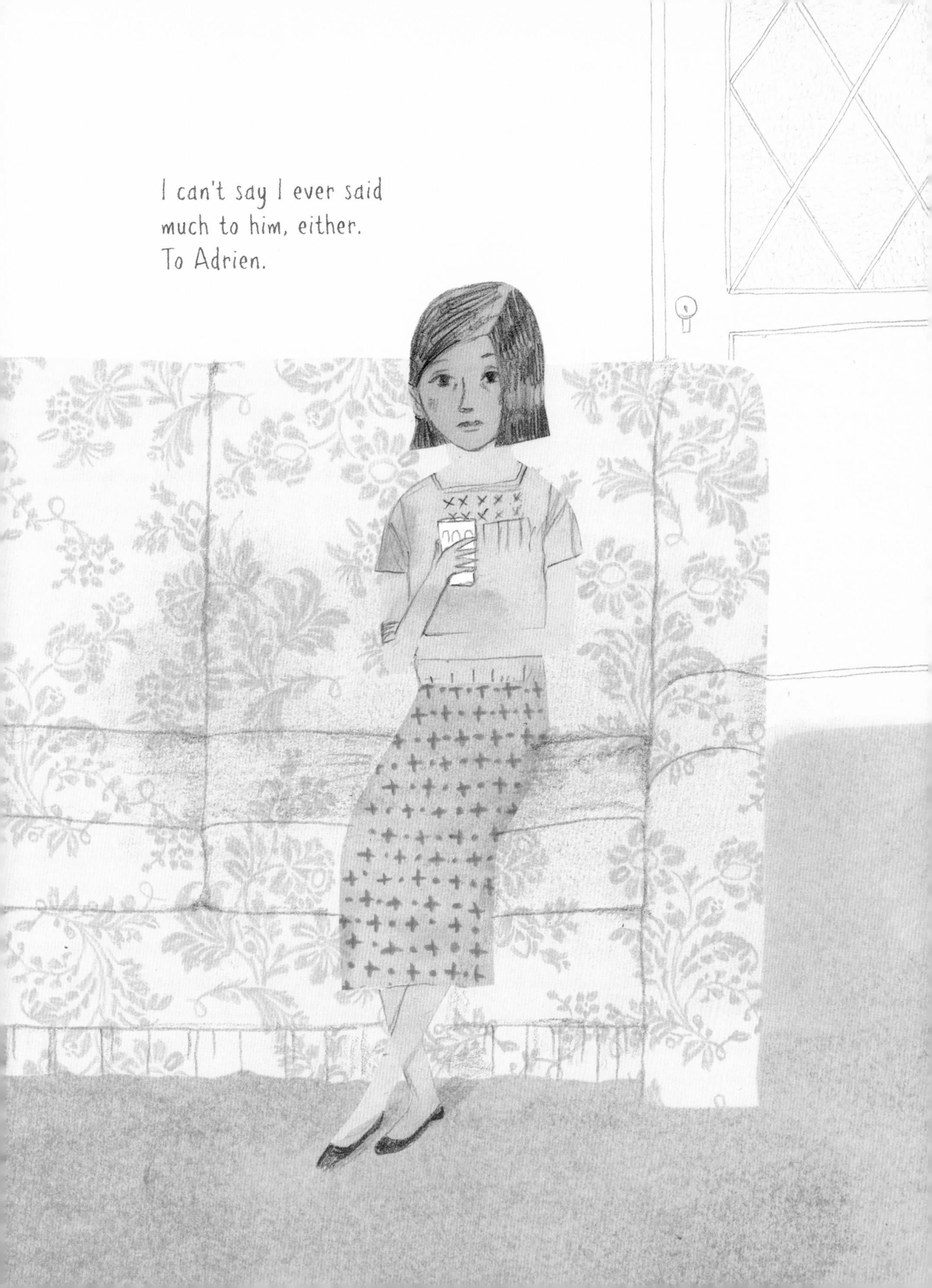

Grandfather always sat next to me at the table.
While everyone else did their thing,
he would quietly take my hand
and hold it.

His own was rough from seventy years
of working at the paper mill,
peeling potatoes in the army,
peeling potatoes for the Brothers.

That's a lot of potato skins
for two hands.

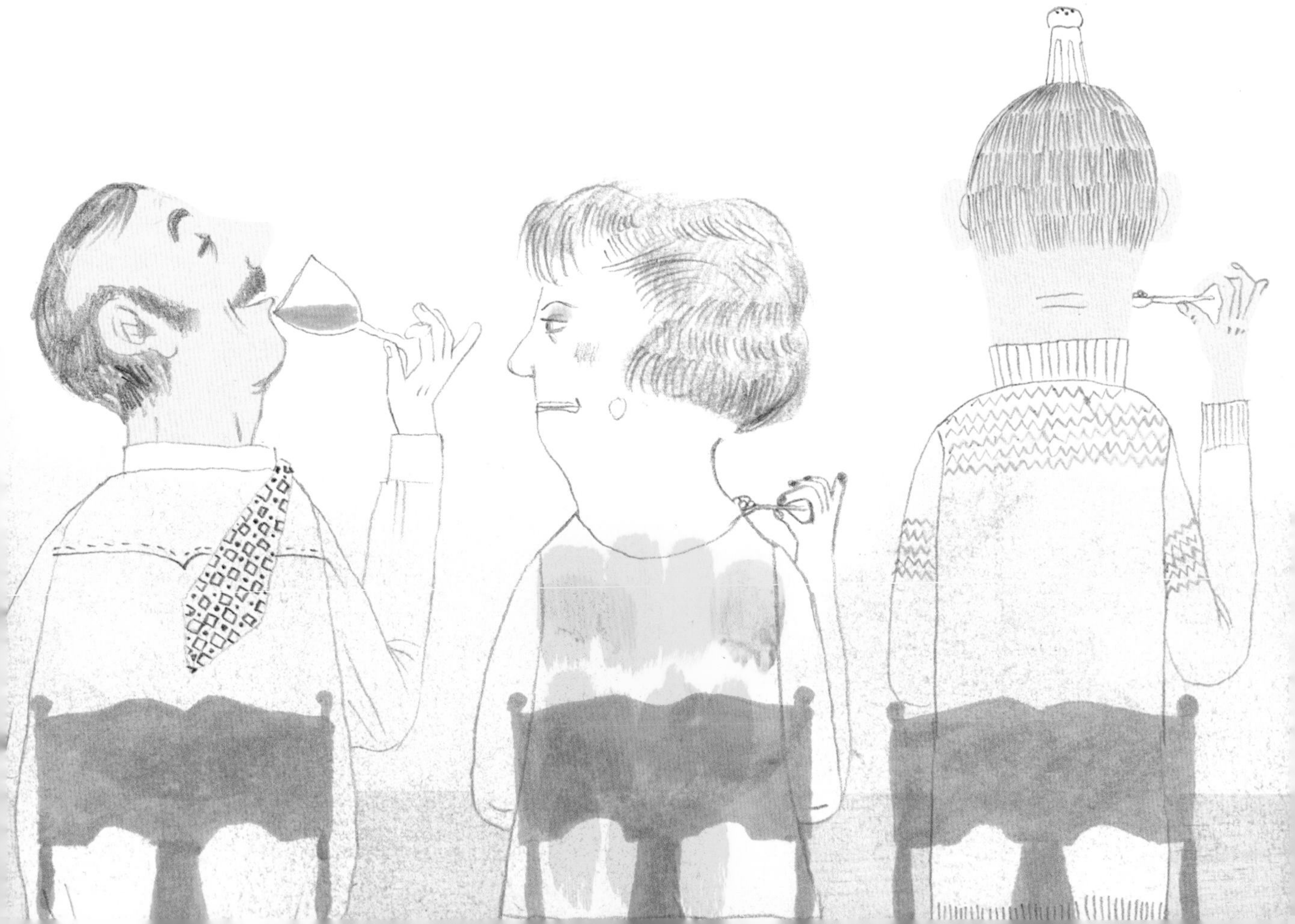

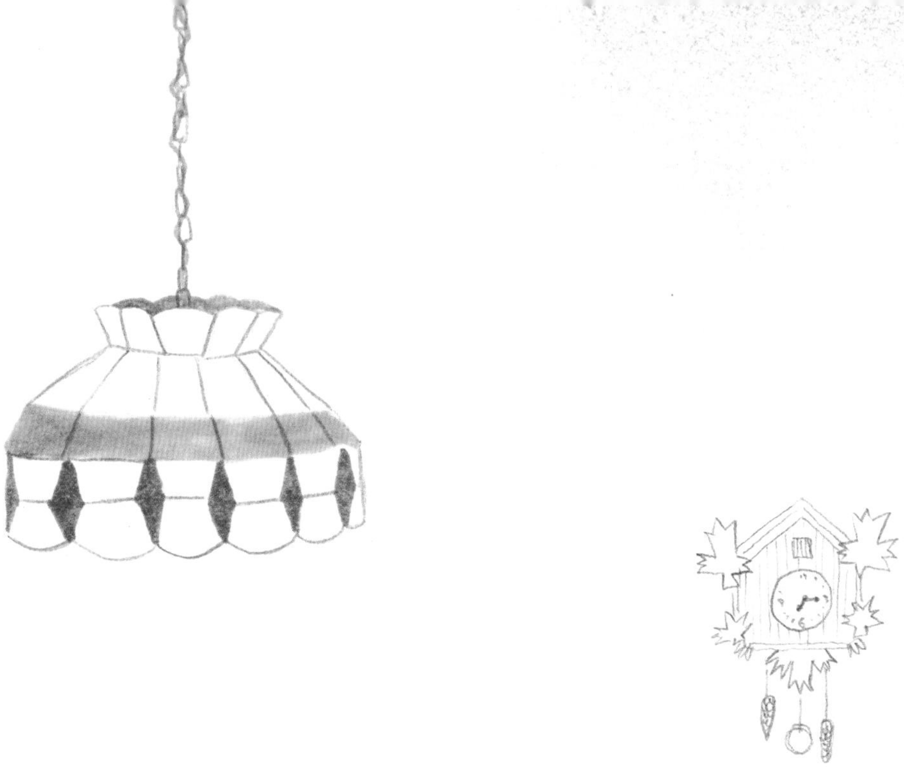

It's so easy not to notice
a man of few words.

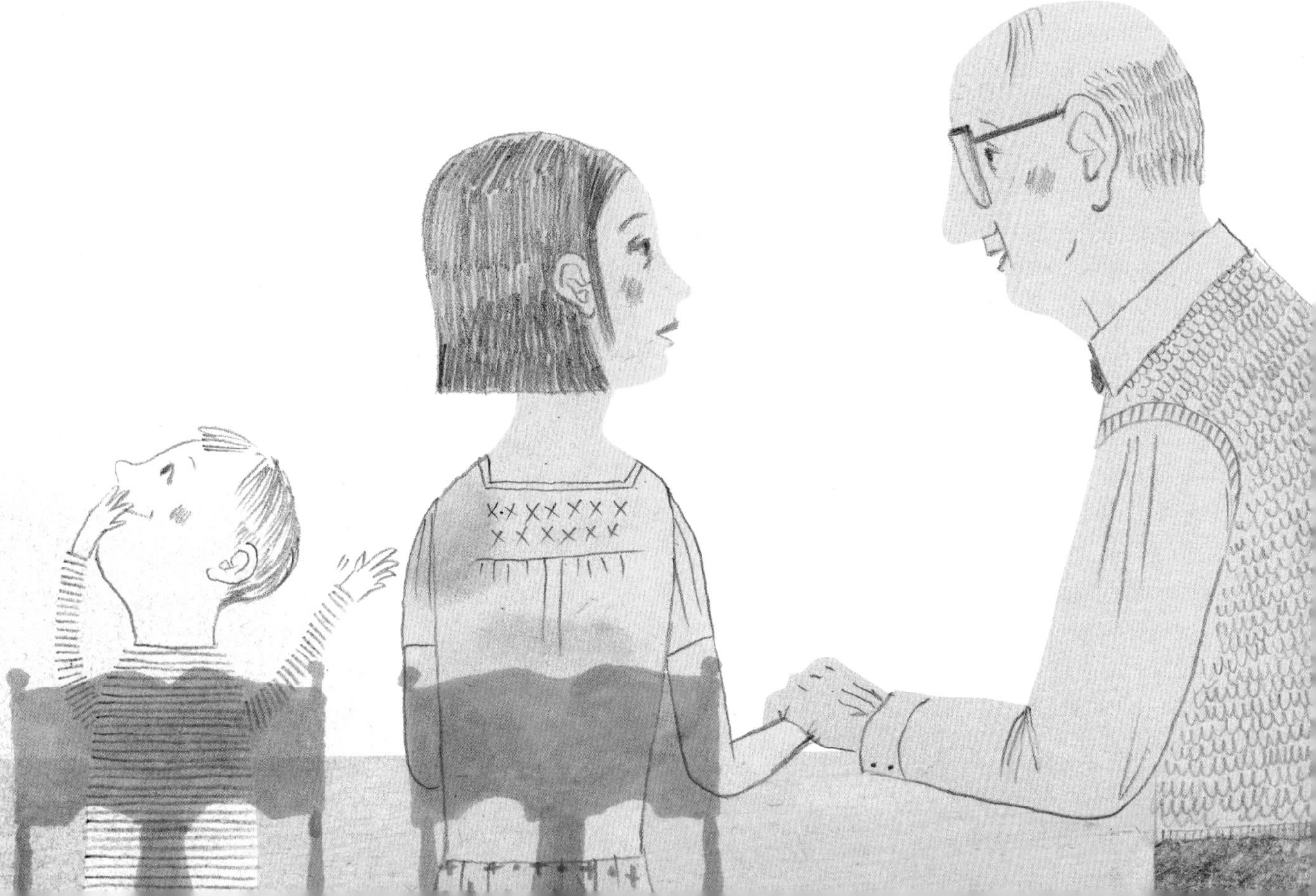

I remember what Adrien liked —

spaghetti out of a can,
forts made out of blankets,
and caramel.
Homemade.

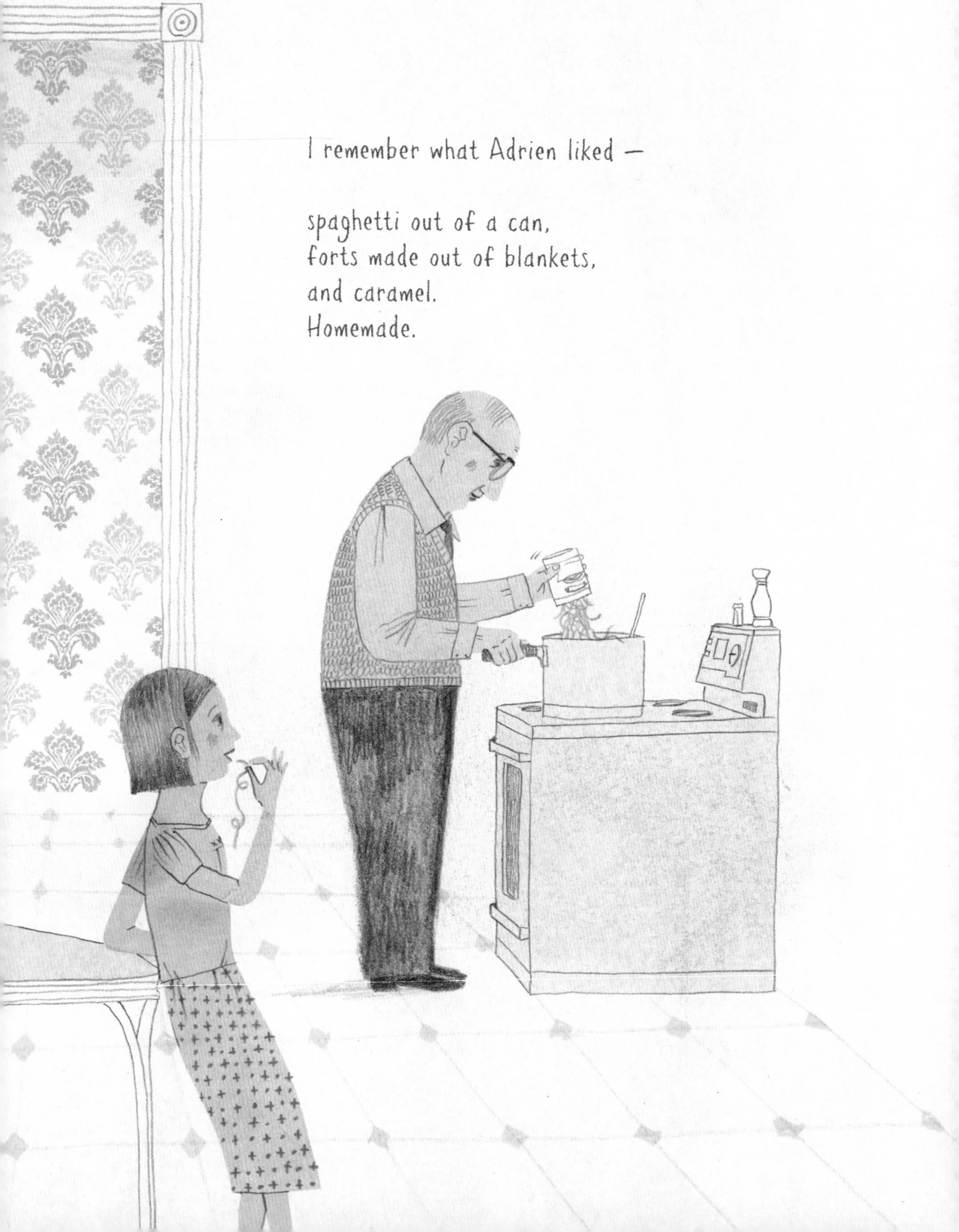

He liked to call me Mémère.

As in,
"Mémère, make sure you go and get yourself a degree."

So I imagined that one day we'd go and get it together,
the way we'd get in his gray Chrysler shaped like a box of soap,
to pick up brown sugar for the caramel.

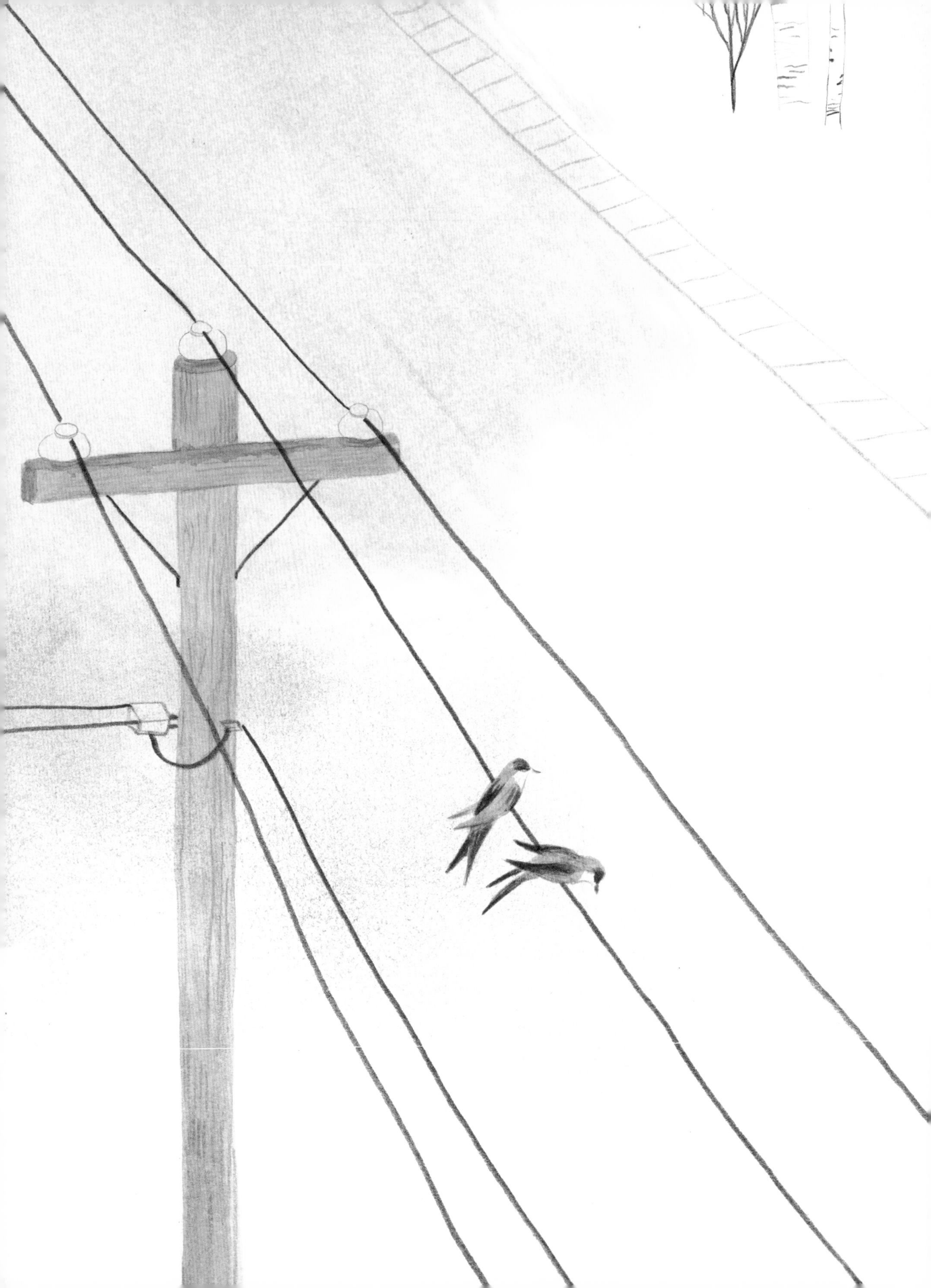

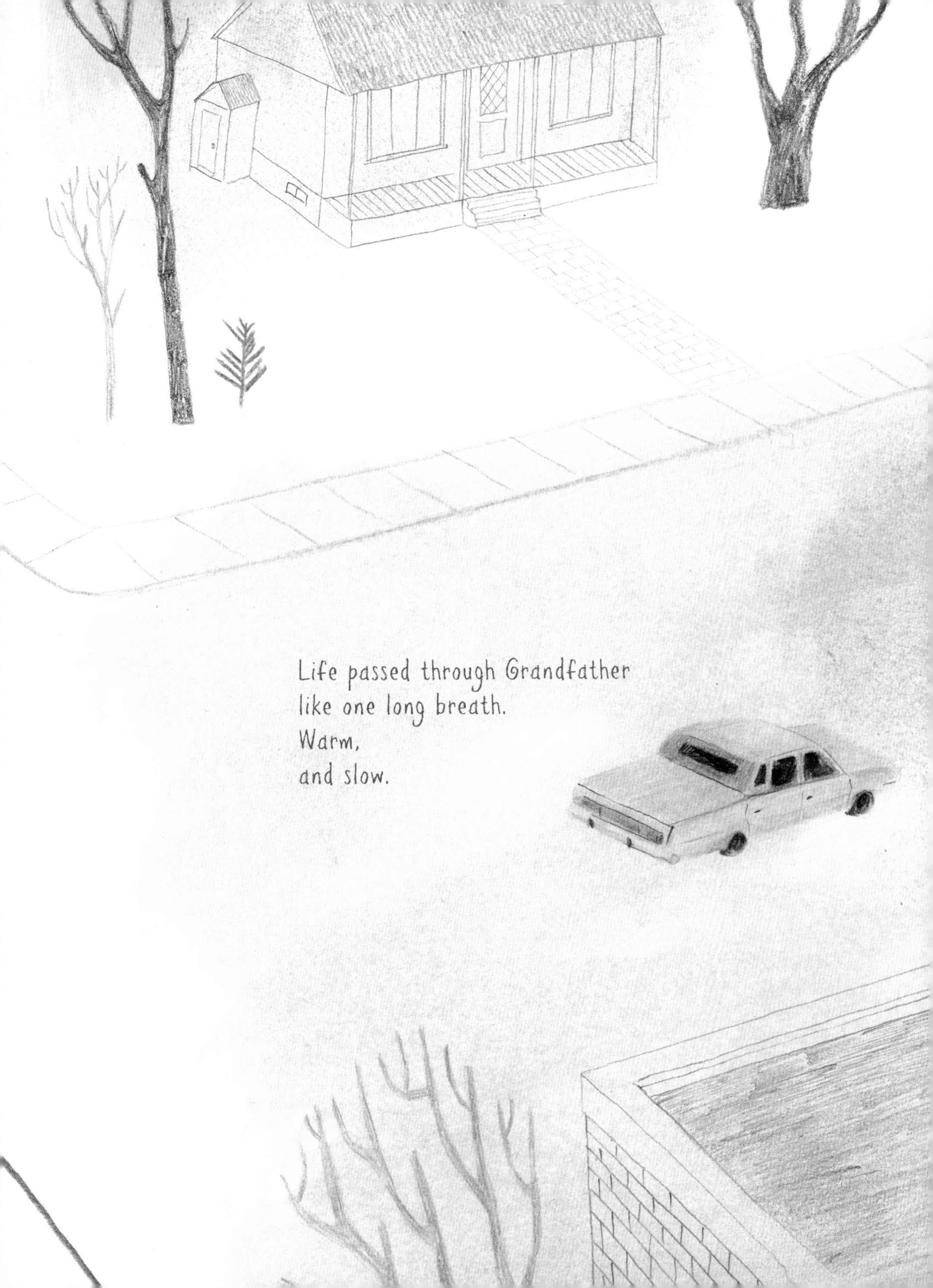

Life passed through Grandfather
like one long breath.
Warm,
and slow.

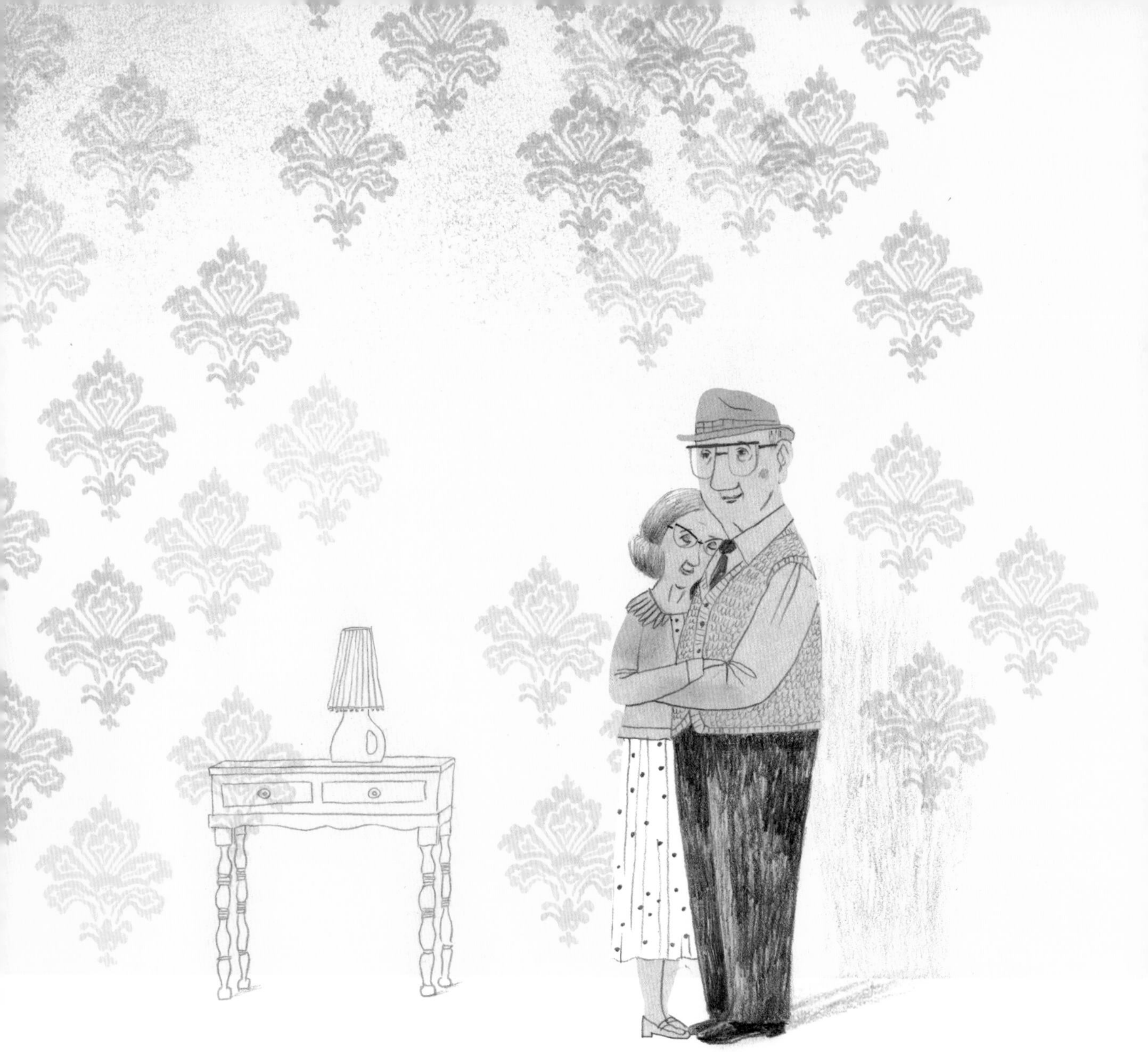

Grandfather loved Lucille.

Not like those old people
who have everything behind them and nothing much
to look forward to
and who stay together
because it's better than being alone.

Grandfather loved Lucille like crazy.

He said things like
"Lucille's waist is the same size as my hatband."

It may seem strange
to compare the love of your life
to your hat,
but it was something he was proud of.

You can't really describe love anyway.
Everyone knows that.

Then
Lucille got cancer.
Lung cancer.

She fought it like crazy.

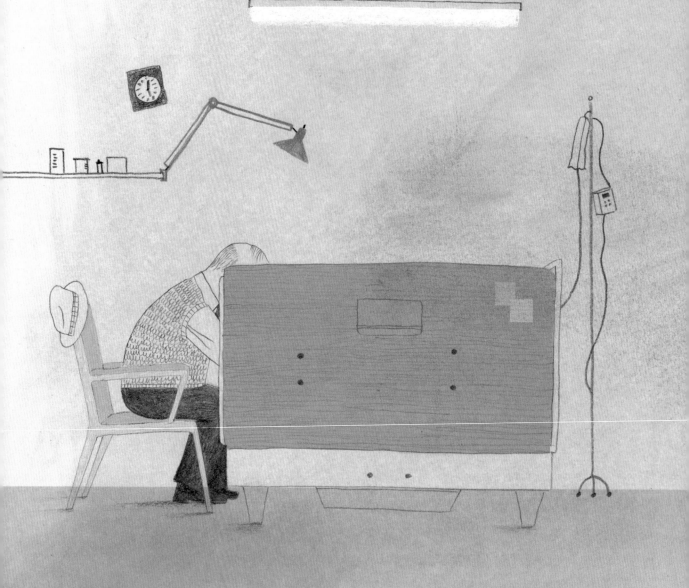

But on one of her not-so-good days, when she was at
the end of her rope and thirsty and her breath was too
short and the rays of sun were too thin in her hospital
room that was too white — all those things that pile up
and kill hope came and settled in for good,
and Lucille passed away.

The life just went out of her.

And with it went the chest pain, the shortness of breath
and even the rays of sunshine that she loved so much.

Everything you could think of.

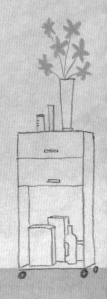

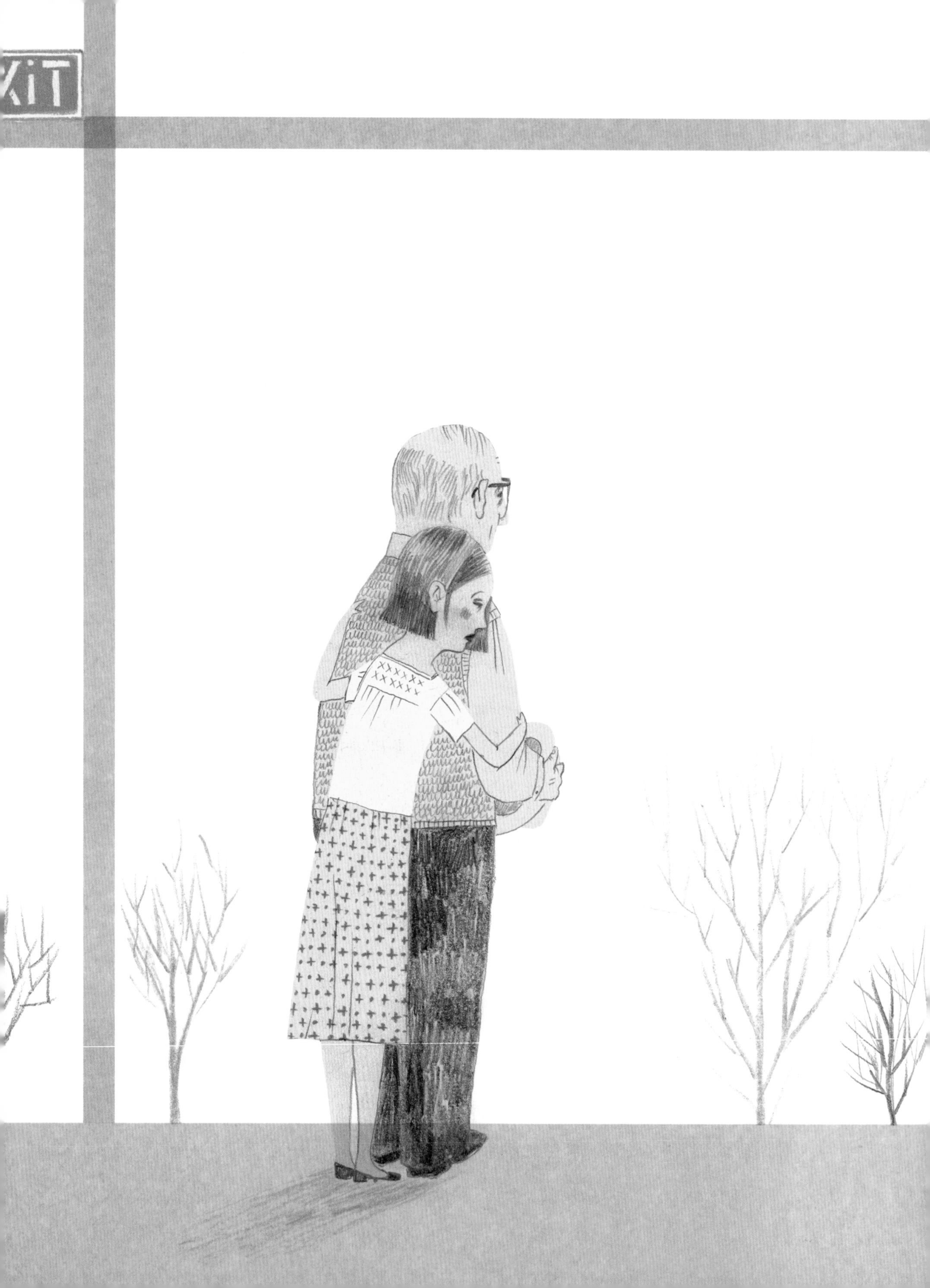
XIT

After that day,
everyone learned to live without Lucille,
because that's what you have to do.

Everyone
except Grandfather.

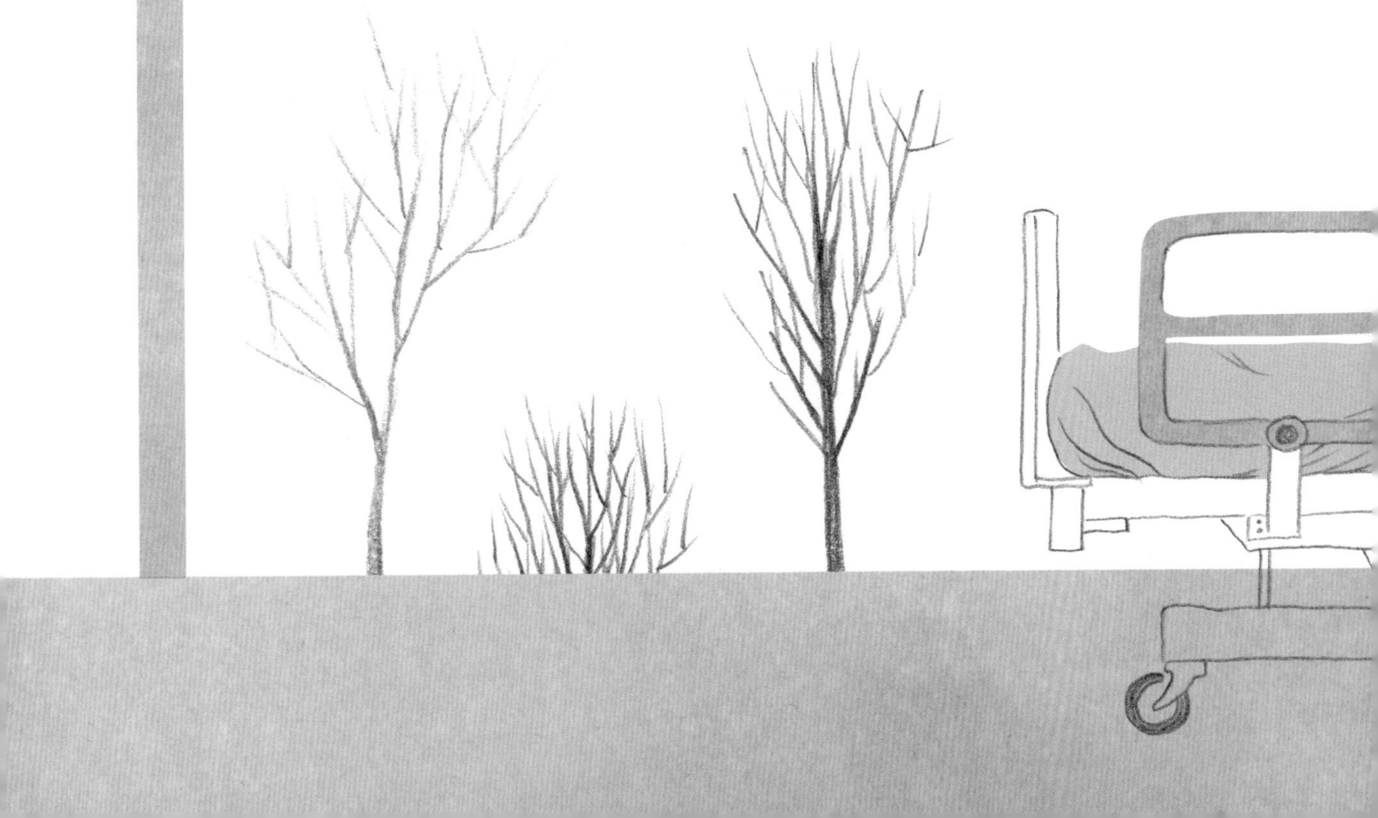

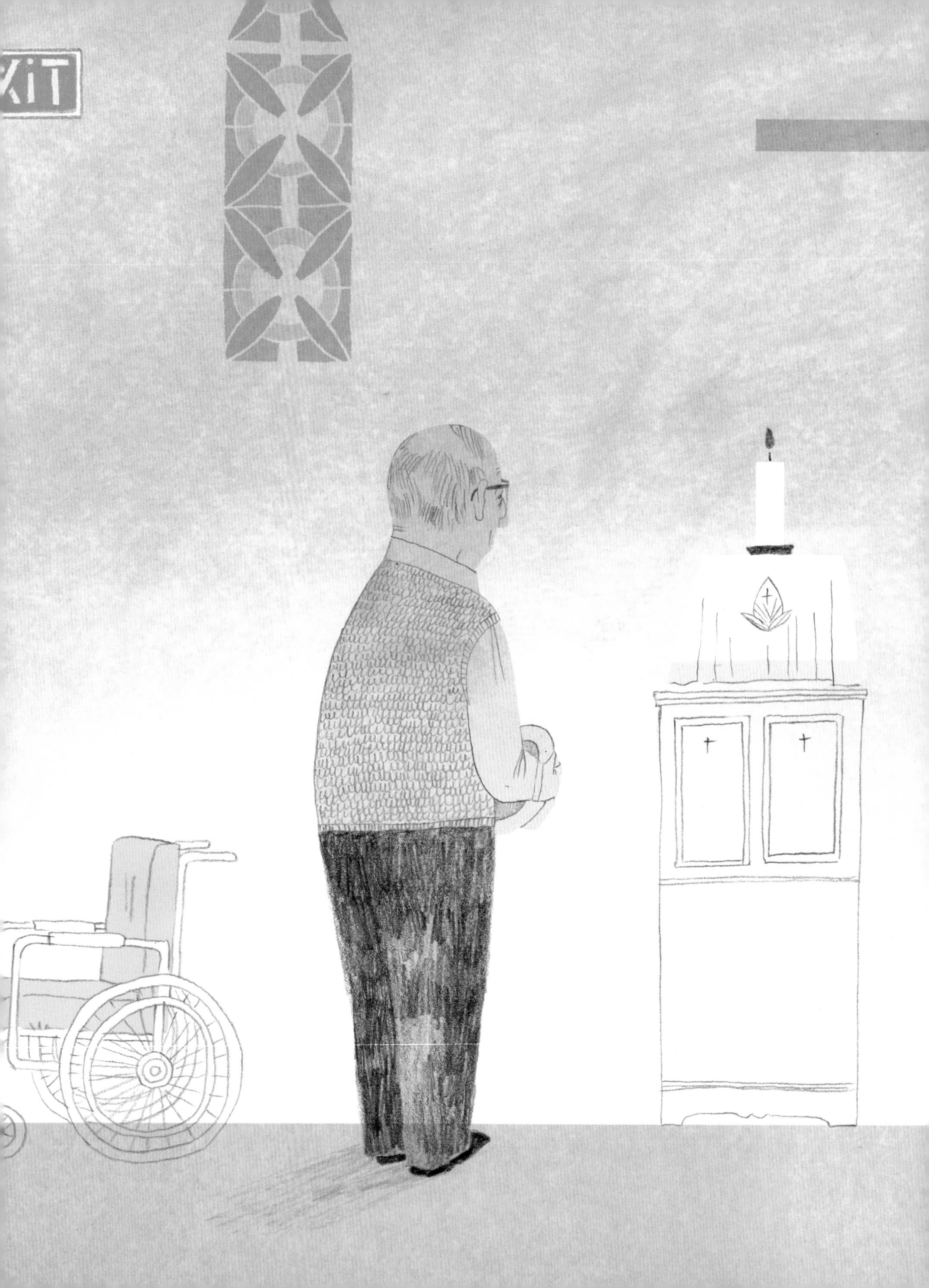
XIT

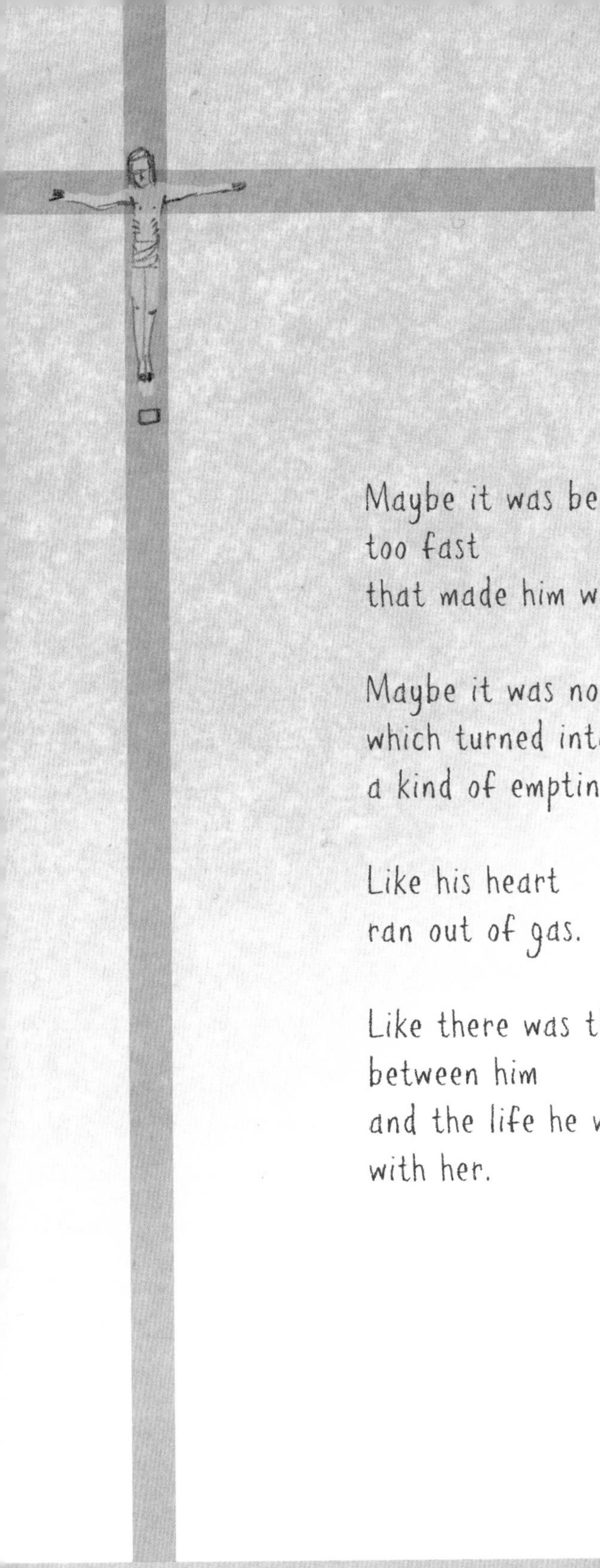

Maybe it was being so sad about losing her
too fast
that made him want to stay silent.

Maybe it was not being able to understand,
which turned into
a kind of emptiness.

Like his heart
ran out of gas.

Like there was this wall
between him
and the life he would have had
with her.

Maybe Grandfather even asked himself
what kind of man he would have been
if Lucille hadn't left without him
that day.

Gone, without him.

(Or if part of him
hadn't left with her.)

Grandfather came to my ballet recital
every year.
The school auditorium was always packed
with parents
proud as peacocks.

The auditorium seated 309 —
308 people
who were proud as peacocks
and one man
who was asleep.

That was Grandfather.

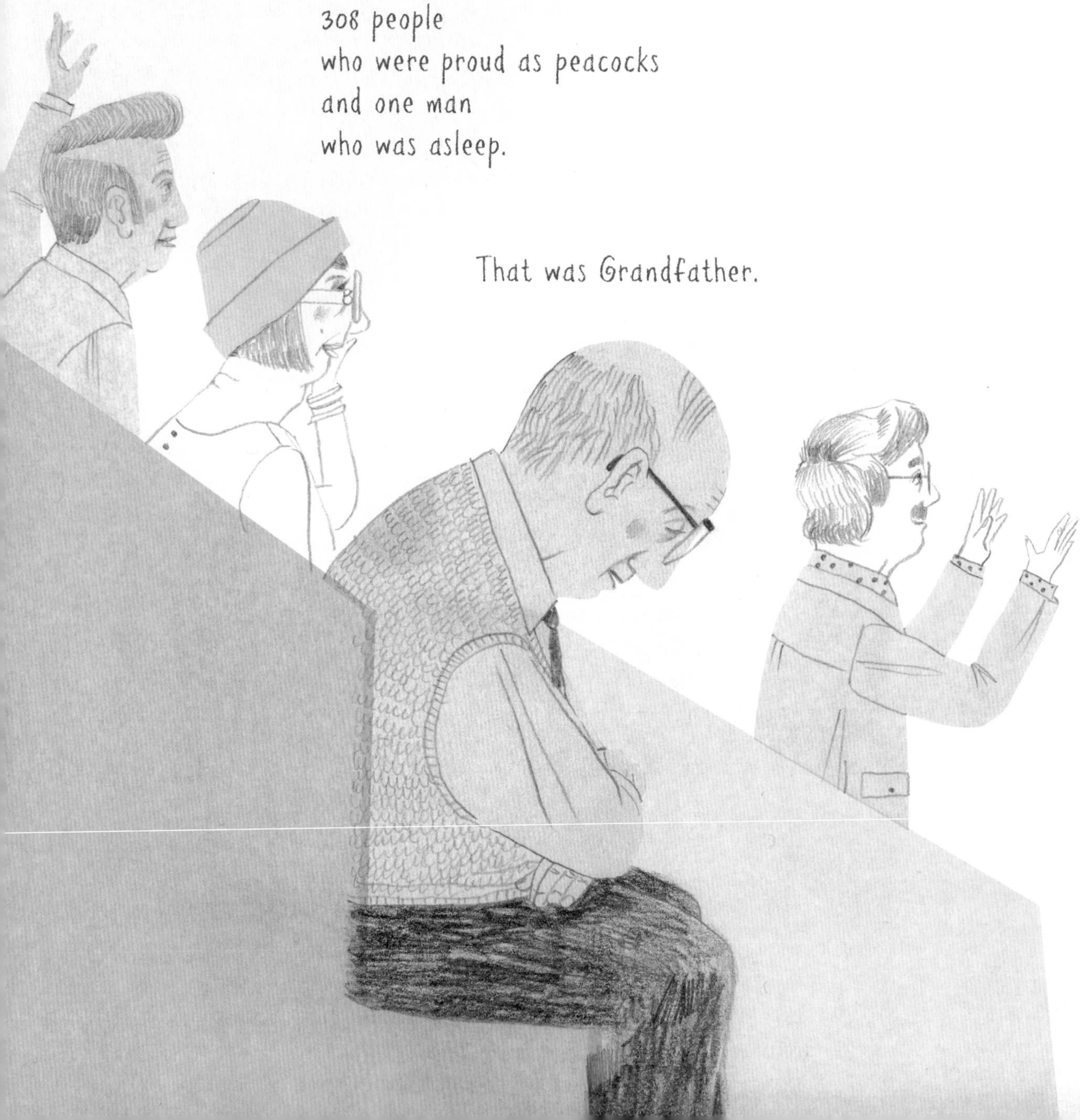

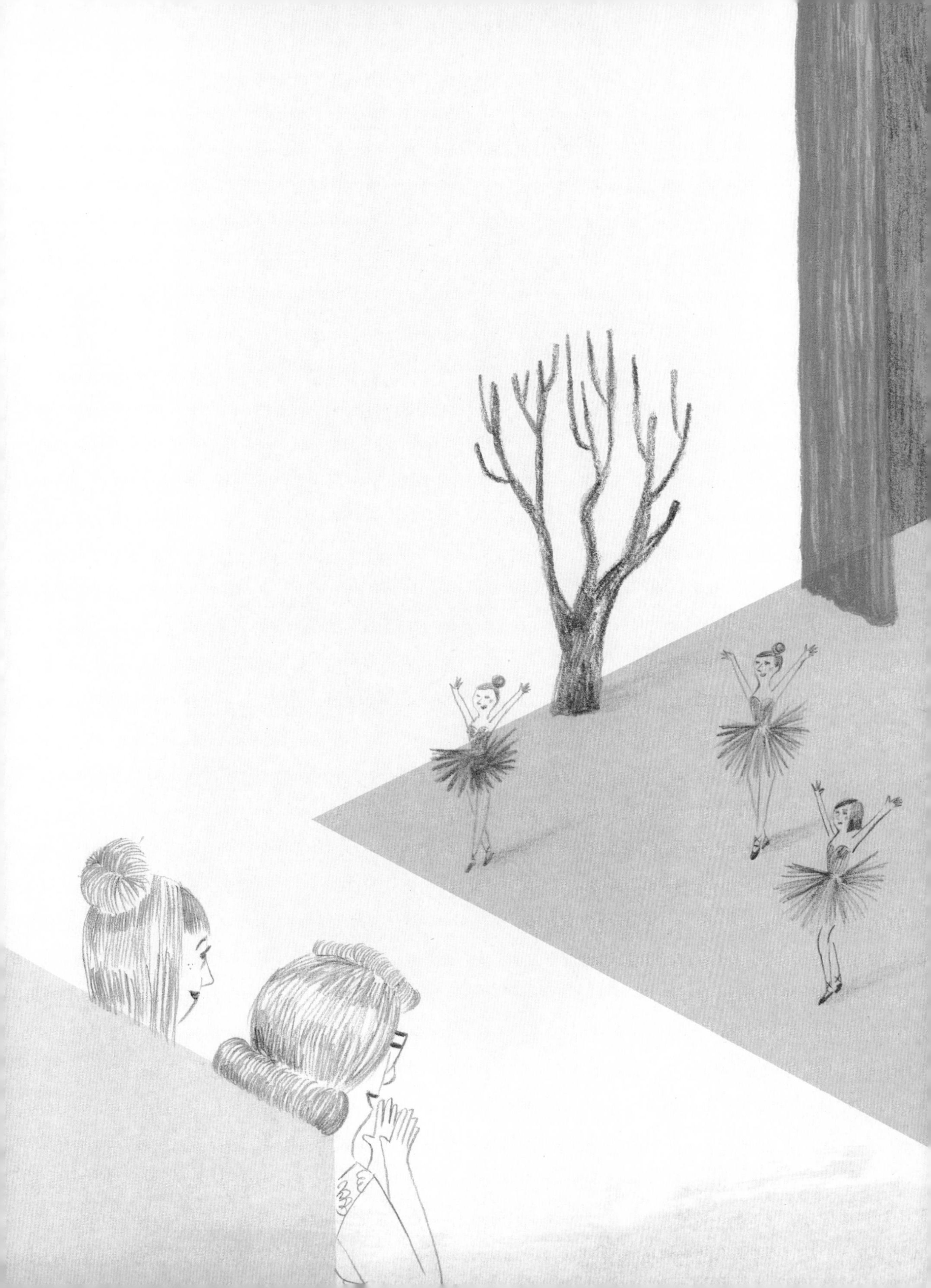

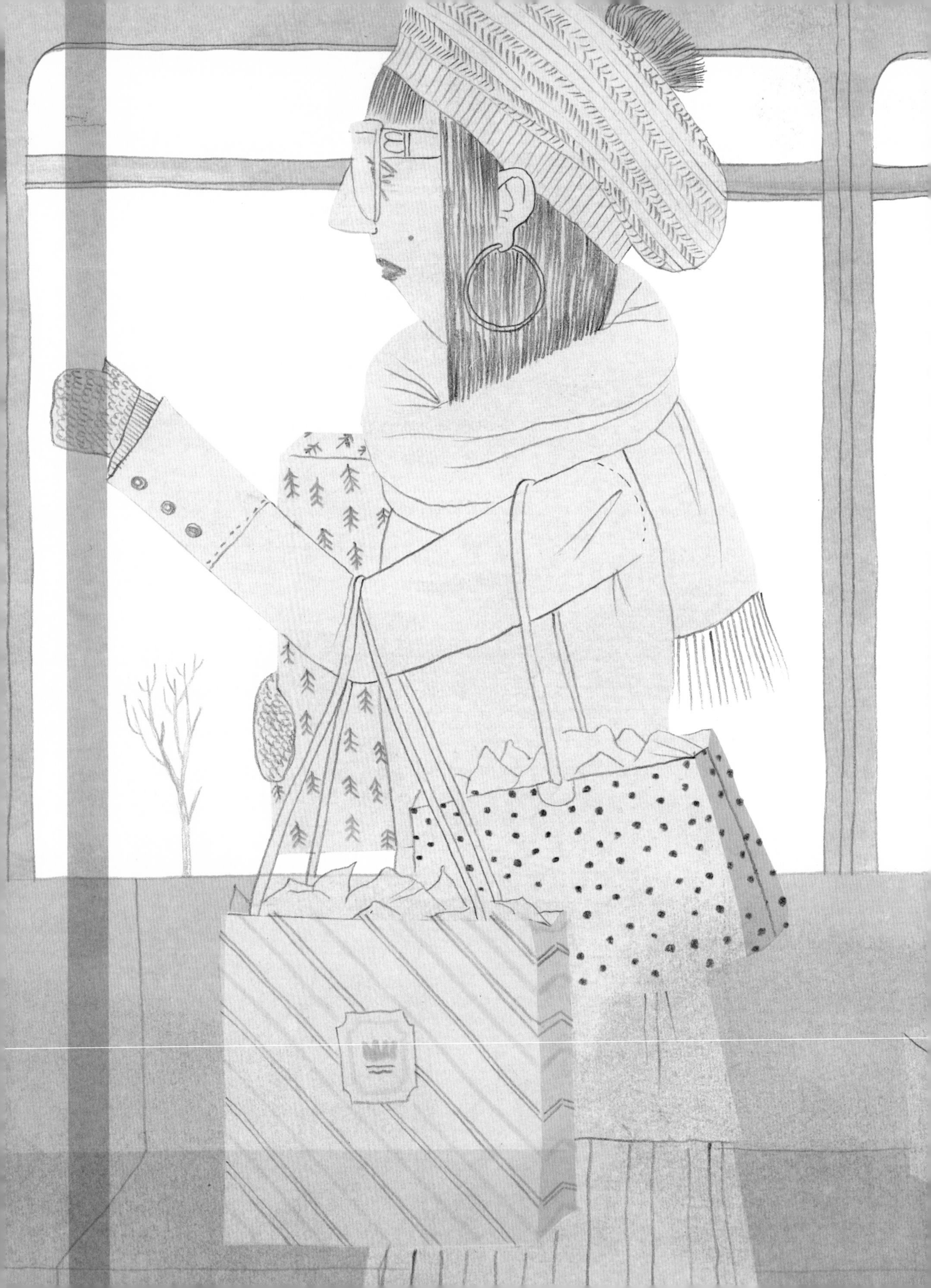

Grandfather also fell asleep in malls,
at the movies, on the bus and at Christmas.

The sights and sounds of the world
didn't interest him much.

"... as long as you get yourself a degree, Mémère."

"Yes, Grandfather."

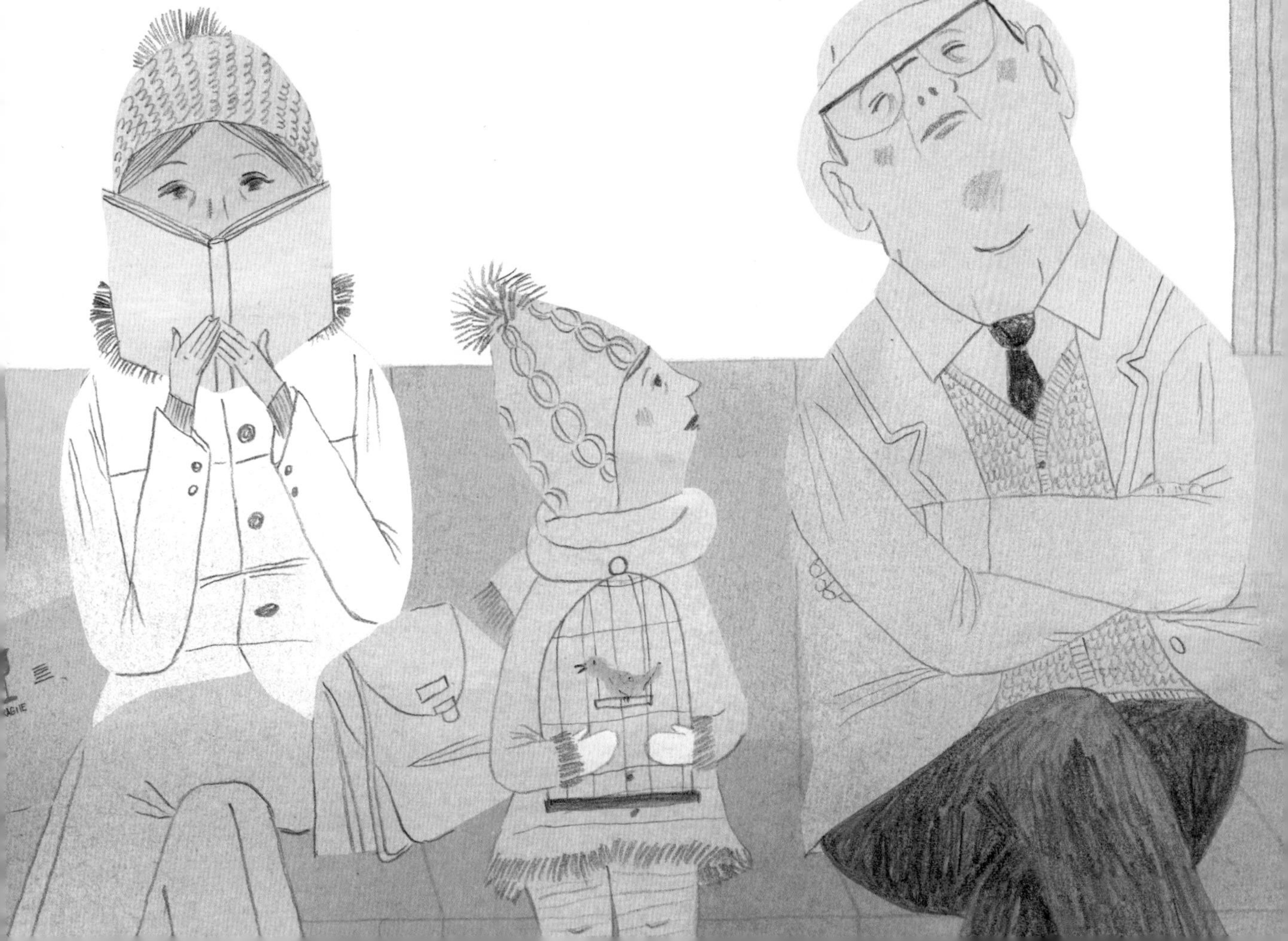

Grandfather was born on August 5, 1930.
The same day as Neil Armstrong.

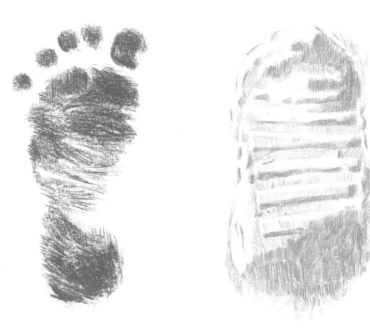

Adrien
August 5, 1930

Neil
August 5, 1930

I thought it would make him proud
when I told him that I'd been chosen for the
Who Will Go to the Moon Contest.

"I'm going to the moon, Grandfather.
Like Neil."

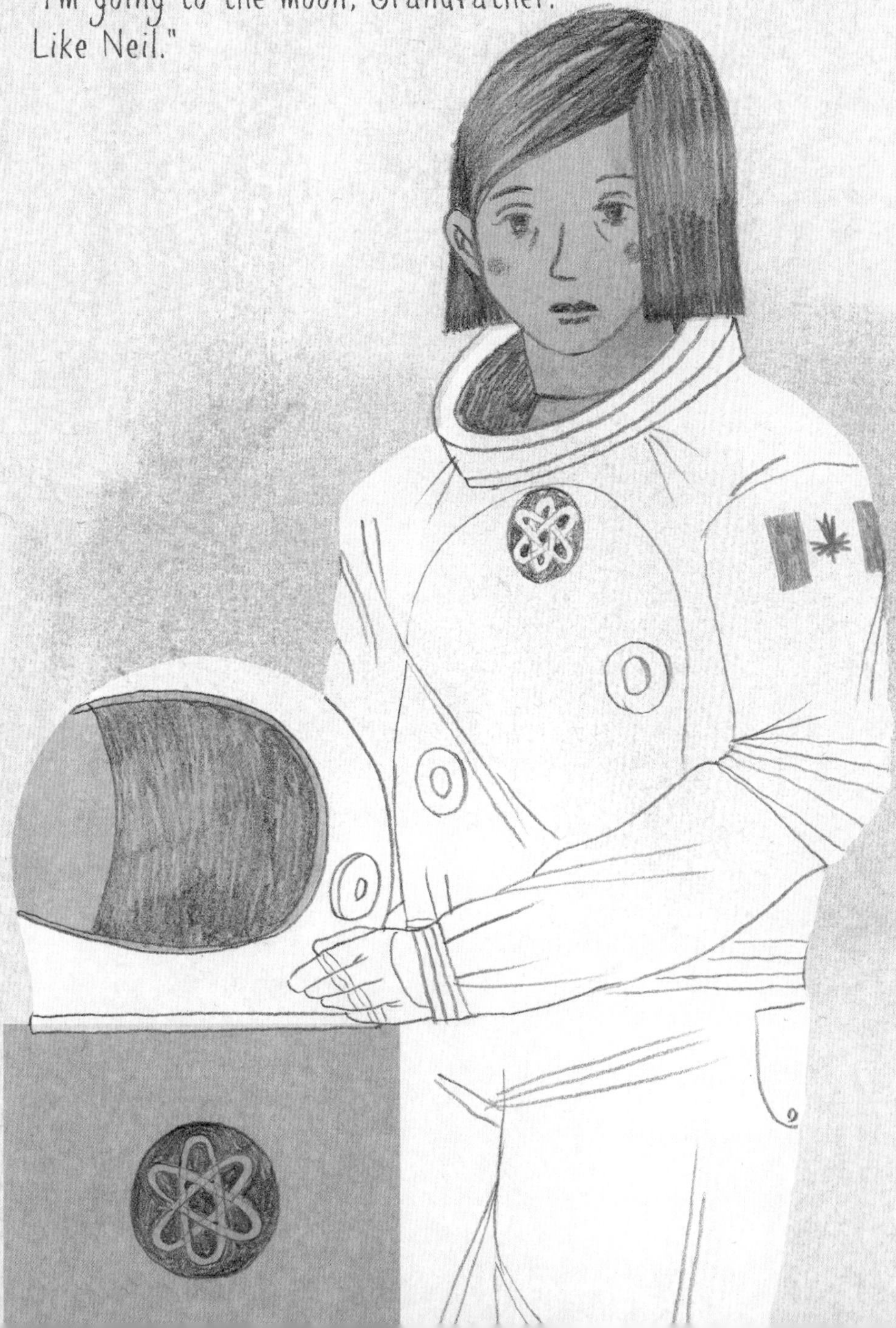

July 20, 1969.
Grandfather was probably sleeping.

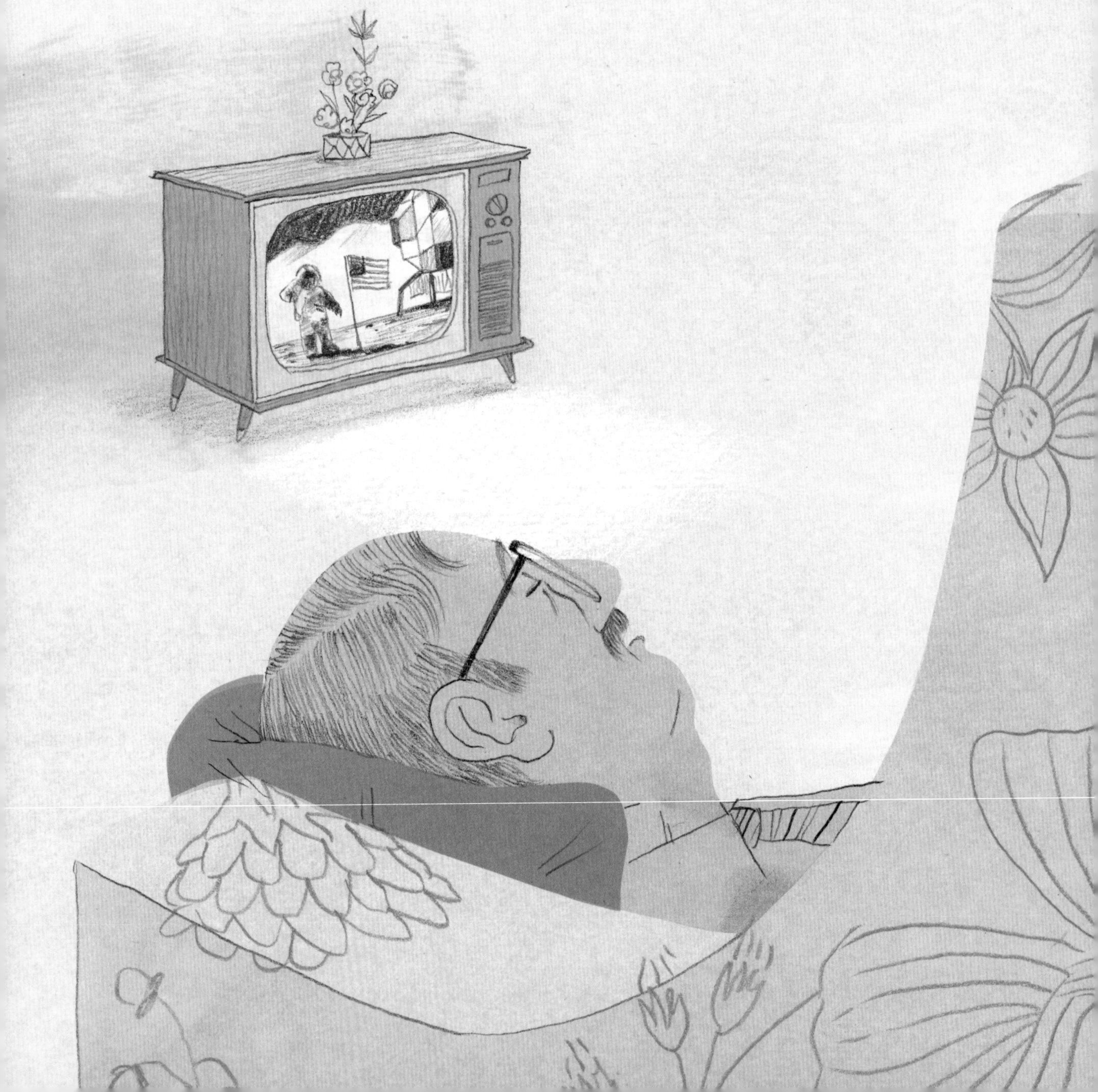

I might as well have been talking to him
about the rain
or the nice weather.

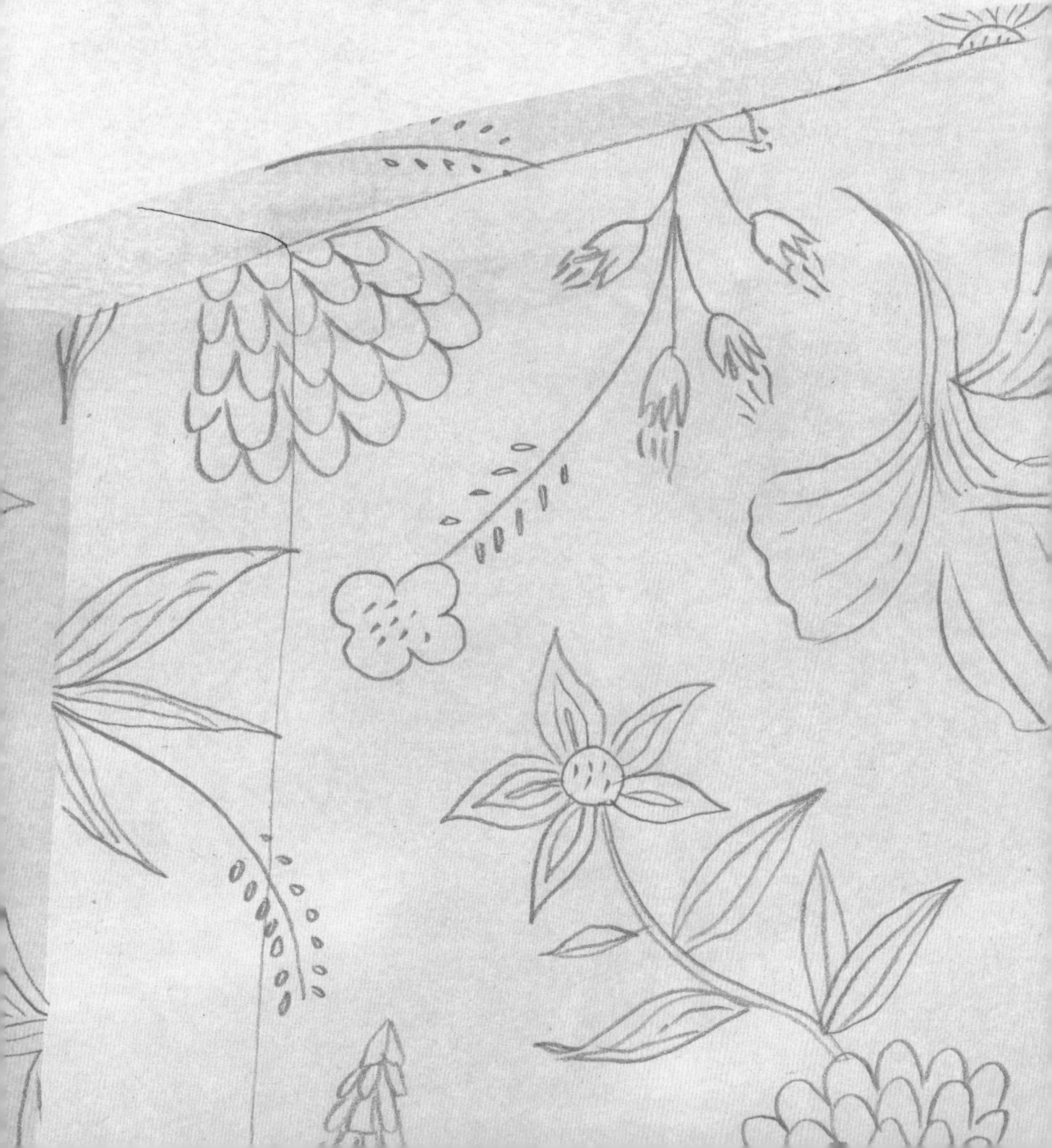

"Don't be scared, Grandfather.
I know it's not like the moon
is just next door.
But these days you can do the return
trip very fast,
and after that, I'm telling you,
everything will be
the way it was before."

He didn't say anything.

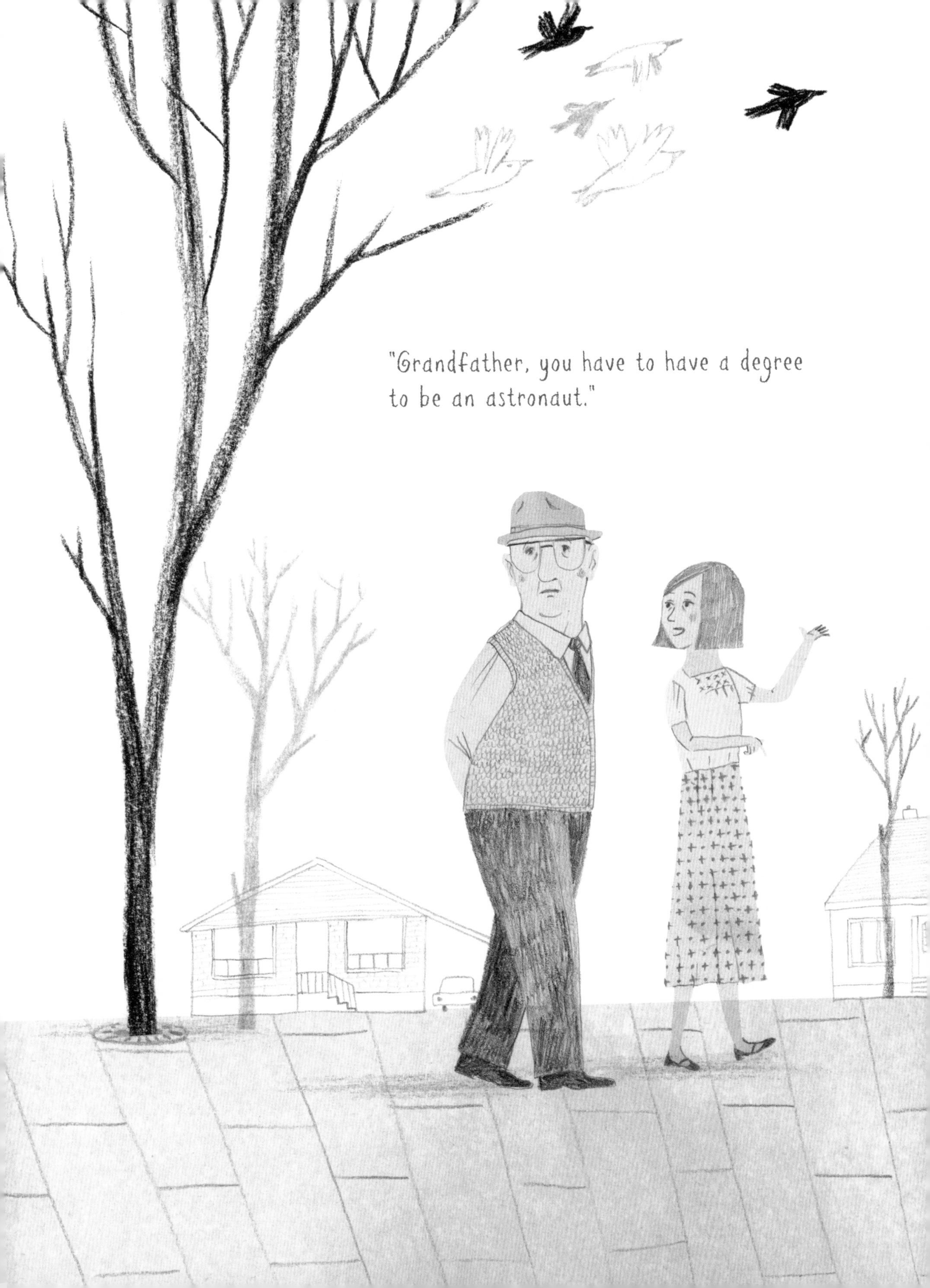

"Grandfather, you have to have a degree to be an astronaut."

Yes, everyone in the whole world
had heard about it.

Everyone knew someone, somewhere,
who had entered the Who Will Go to the Moon Contest.

(Apparently there was even a contestant
from the Republic of Nauru.
That's the smallest country in the world,
with an area of 21 square kilometers.)

Everyone in the whole world
had heard about it.

But not Grandfather,
who didn't watch a lot of TV.

"Television is something that ends up
doing our thinking for us,"
he said.

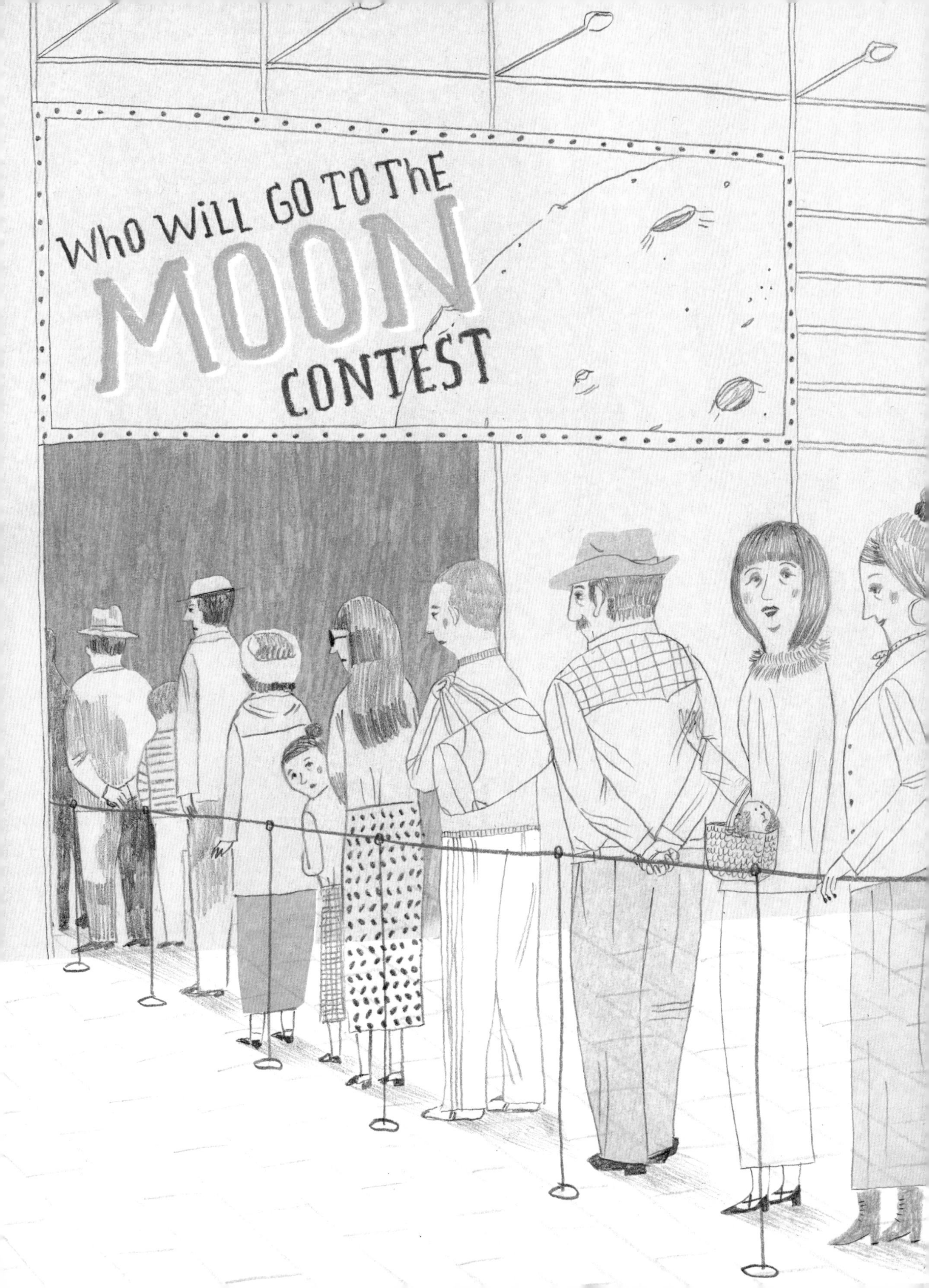
Who Will GO TO The
MOON
CONTEST

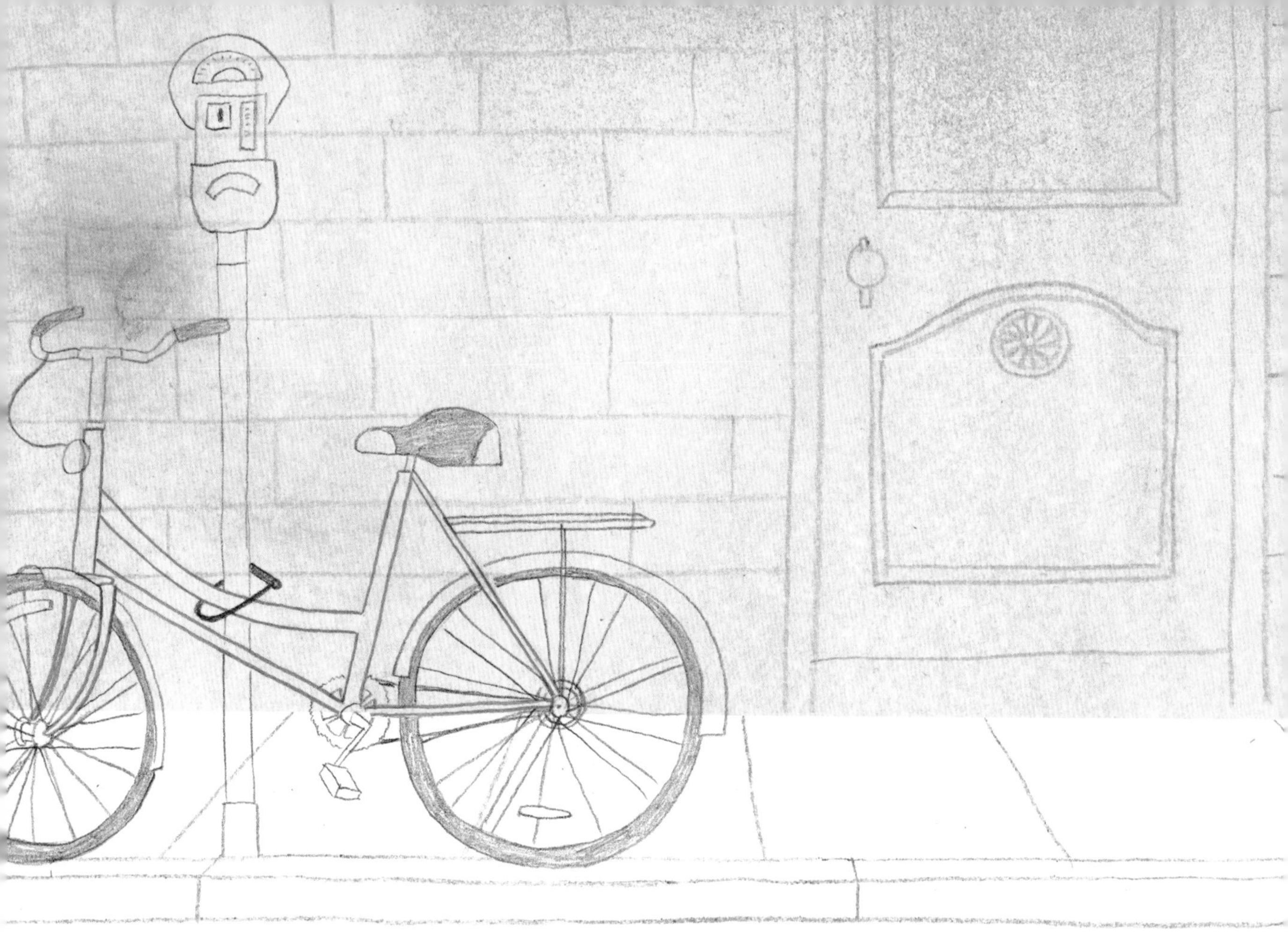

I didn't want my life to be one long breath.
Warm,
and slow.

So I went and took a number
and stood in line.

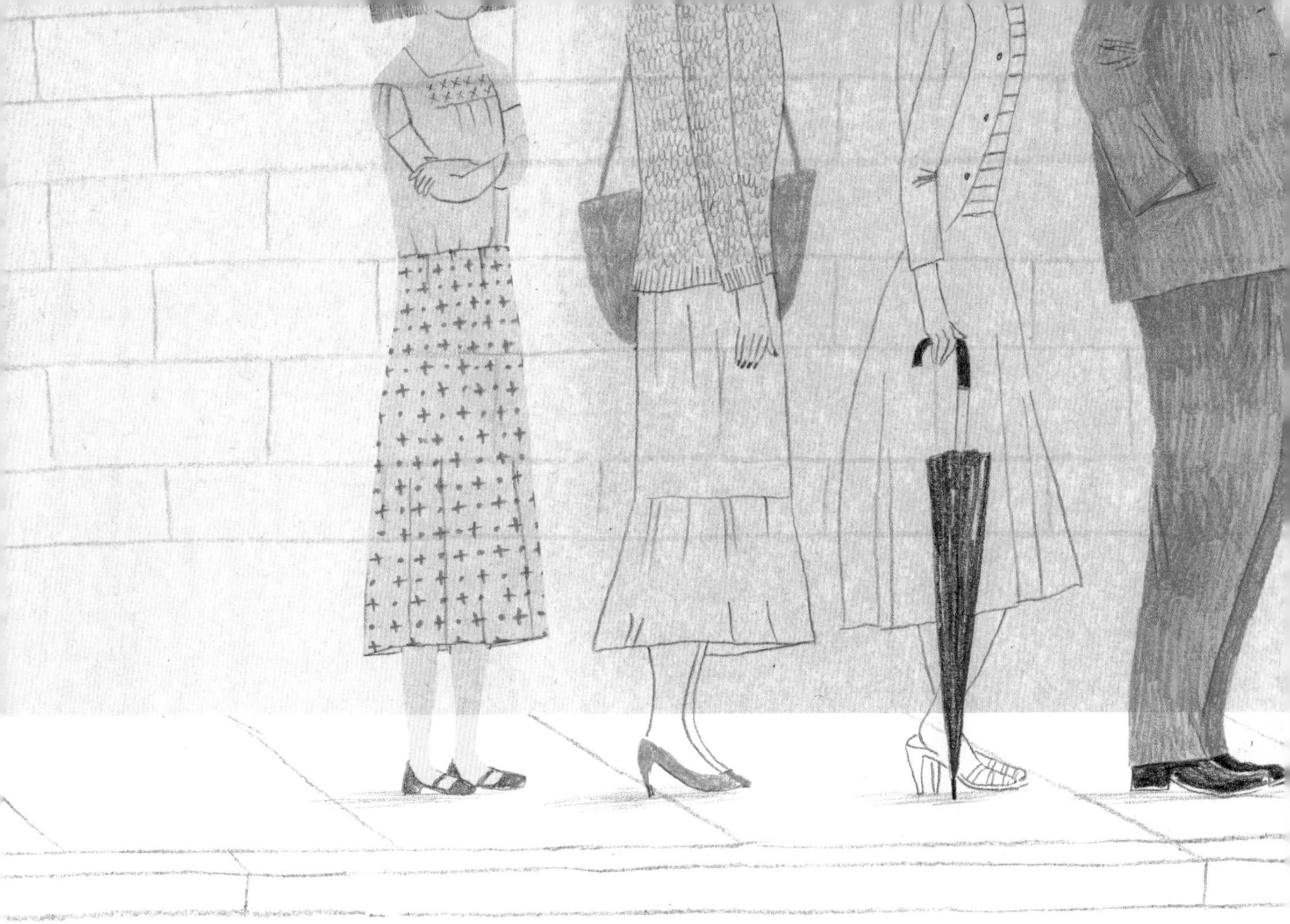

Number 6506

A line
219,191 people long.

It was like the north and south ends of the city
joined hands for once.

It was a bit like those ants
that make their way along the cracks in the sidewalk
without really knowing why,
but just because the one in front moves ahead,
so does the next one
and then the one after that.

They said a lot of true things and a lot of false things
that day.
But the fact remains that the whole city
came to a standstill.
The bridges and the highways and the airports
were all closed.

So that even those who had no interest
in the whole business
had their noses rubbed in it
sooner or later.

Grandfather, for example
(for the first time since Lucille died),
was not able to visit Monsieur Gilbert
as he had done every Tuesday at eleven o'clock.

His barber.

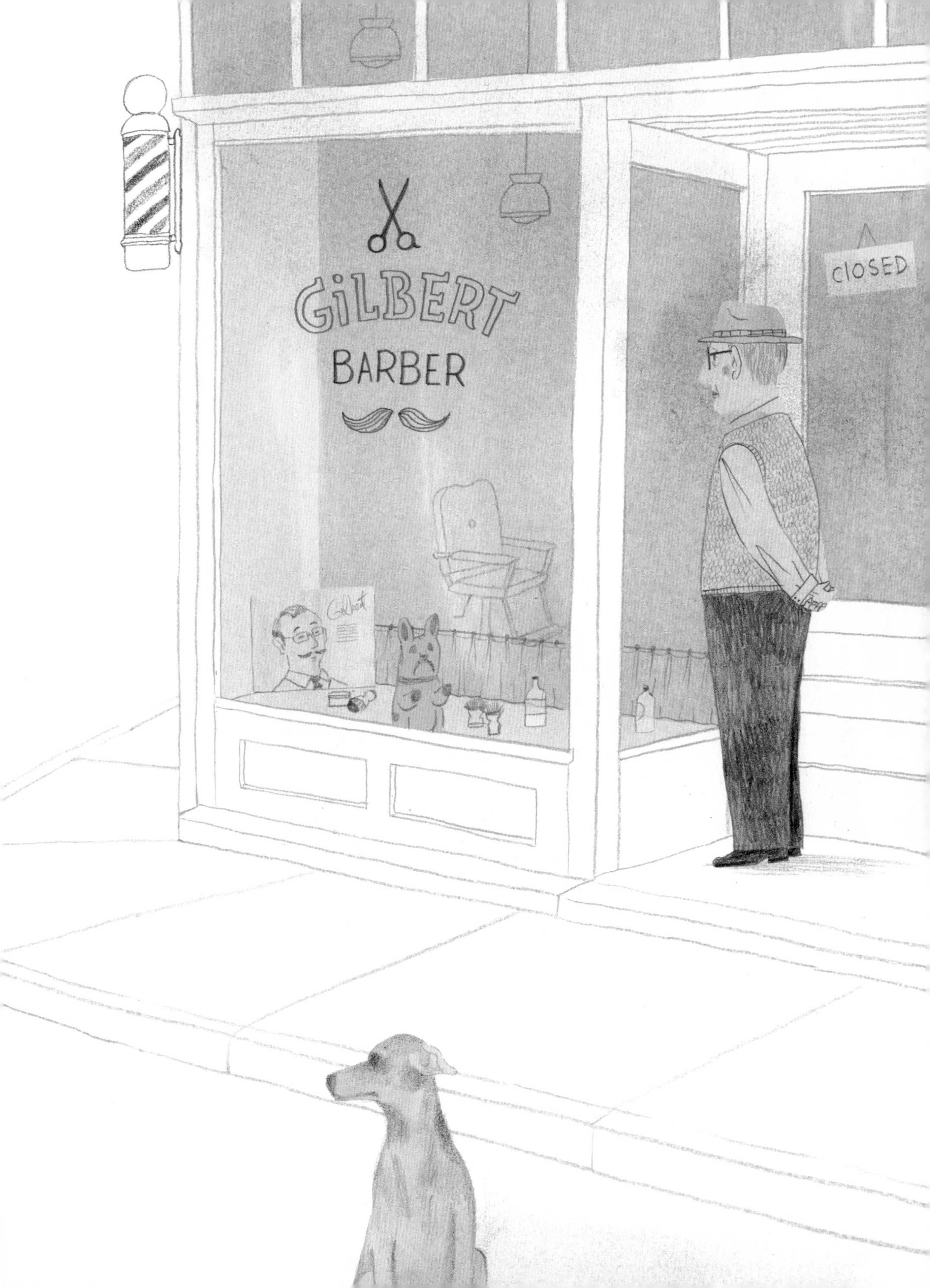
GiLBERT
BARBER
CLOSED
Gilbert

Monsieur Gilbert was standing in line.

It was nice to see
all those faces
looking their best,
wearing the same smile.

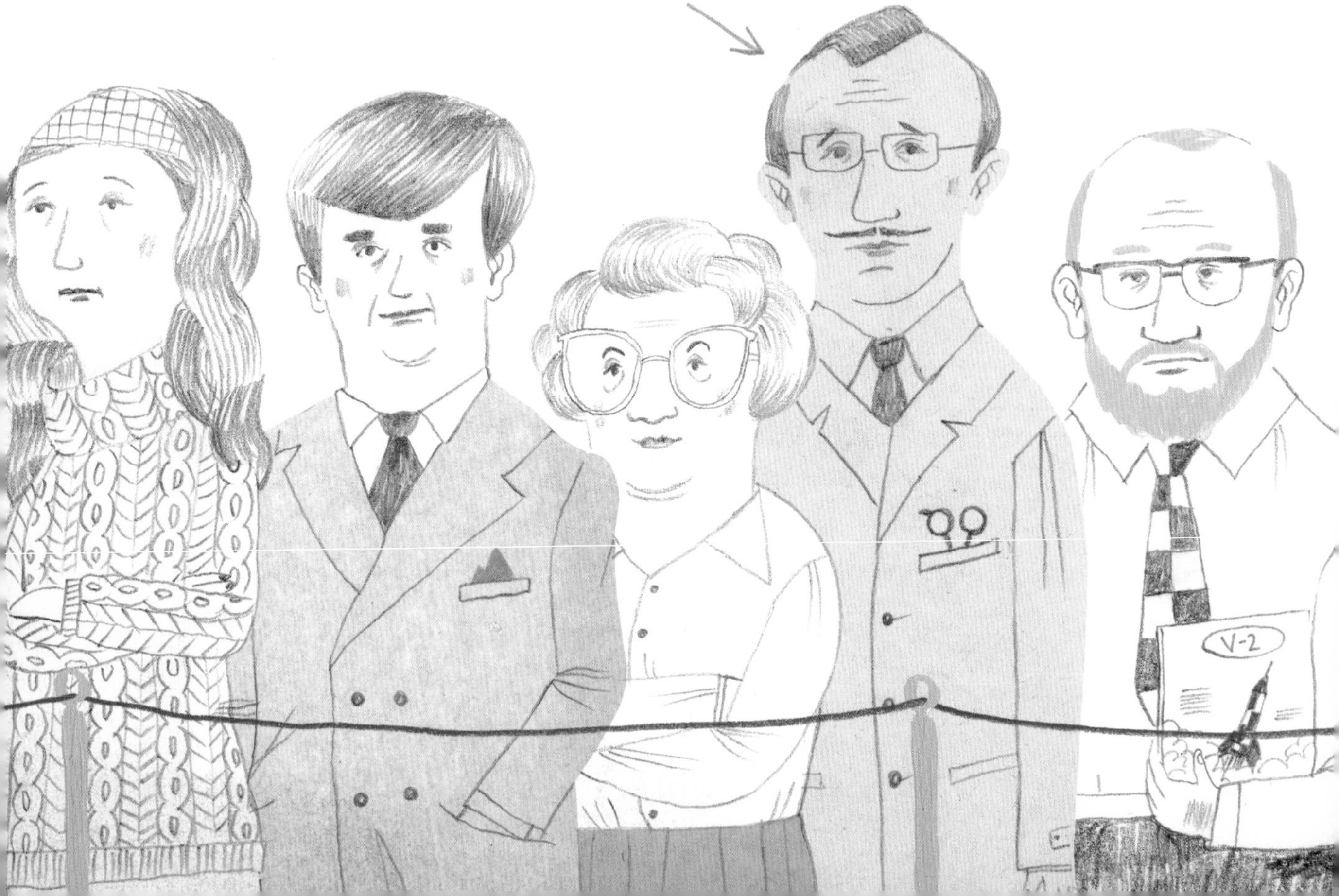
V-2

The smile
of someone who thinks
they're about to win the lottery.

Someone who will finally be able
to leave their life
behind.

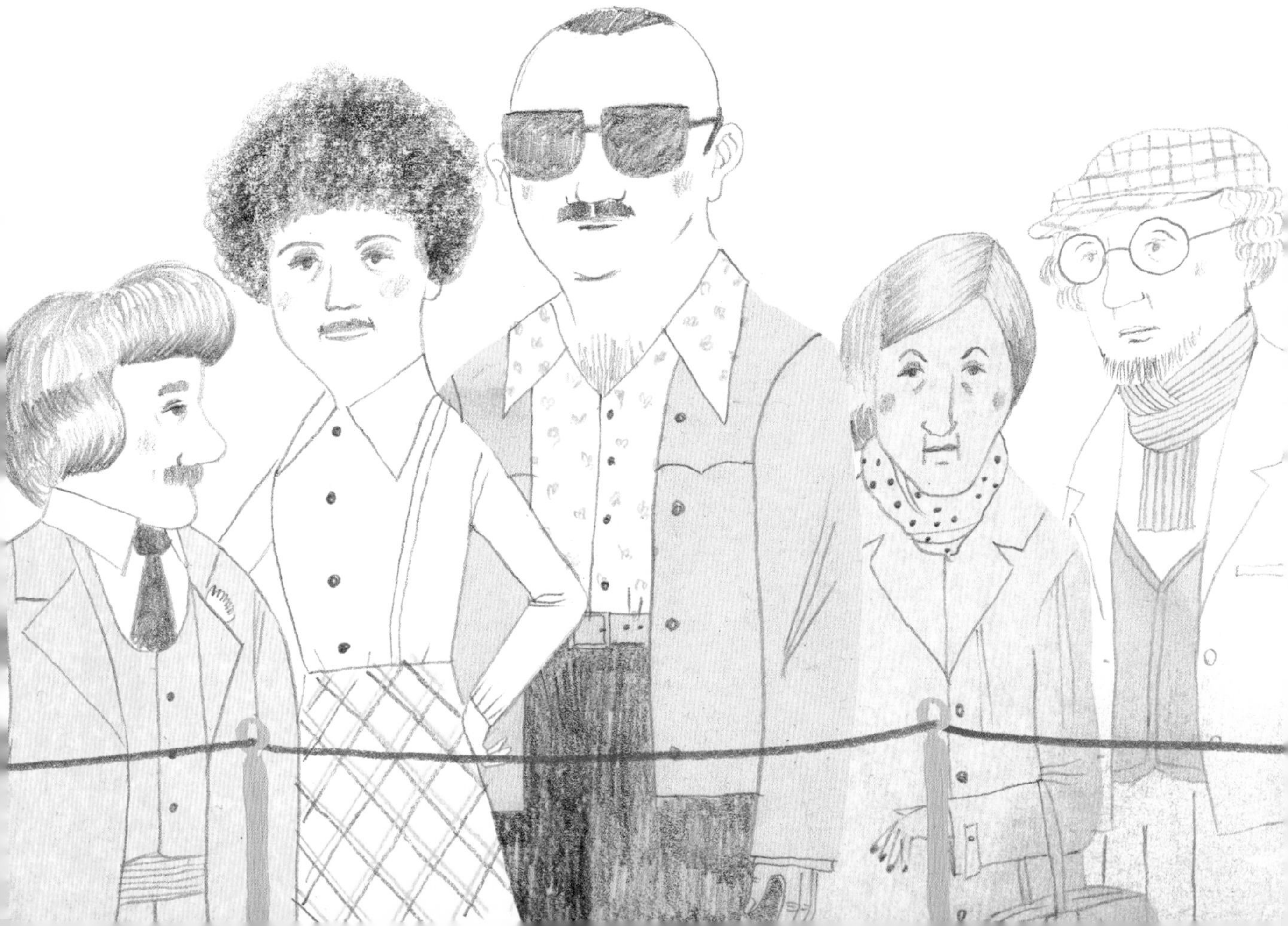

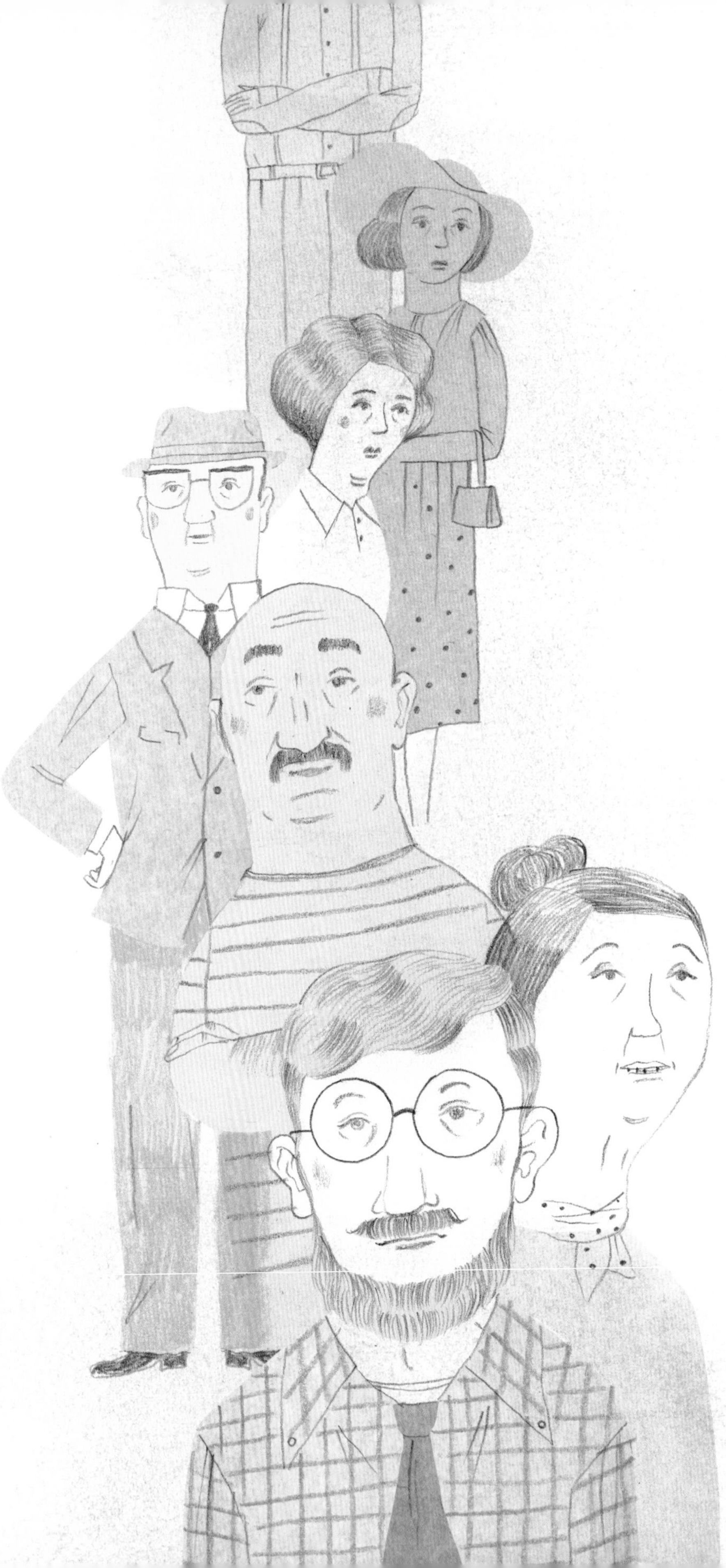

You can't imagine how many people
dream
about going to the moon.

In line stood ...

a red-headed man with round glasses like John Lennon,
a skinny guy with legs at least two meters long,
a woman wearing braces and a sad smile.

I don't know why
they chose me
that day.

I'm not very beautiful
or very ugly.
I'm not very brave.

Maybe they were
actually looking for
someone ordinary.

Maybe it's extraordinary
to send an ordinary person
to the moon.

But I wasn't thinking about any of that
the morning of the launch.

First I have to say
that I forget a lot
about what happened
that morning.

They say it's your memory playing tricks on you.
It's your mind that does it,
to stop your heart
from freaking out.

(The memory lapses
keep things
on track.)

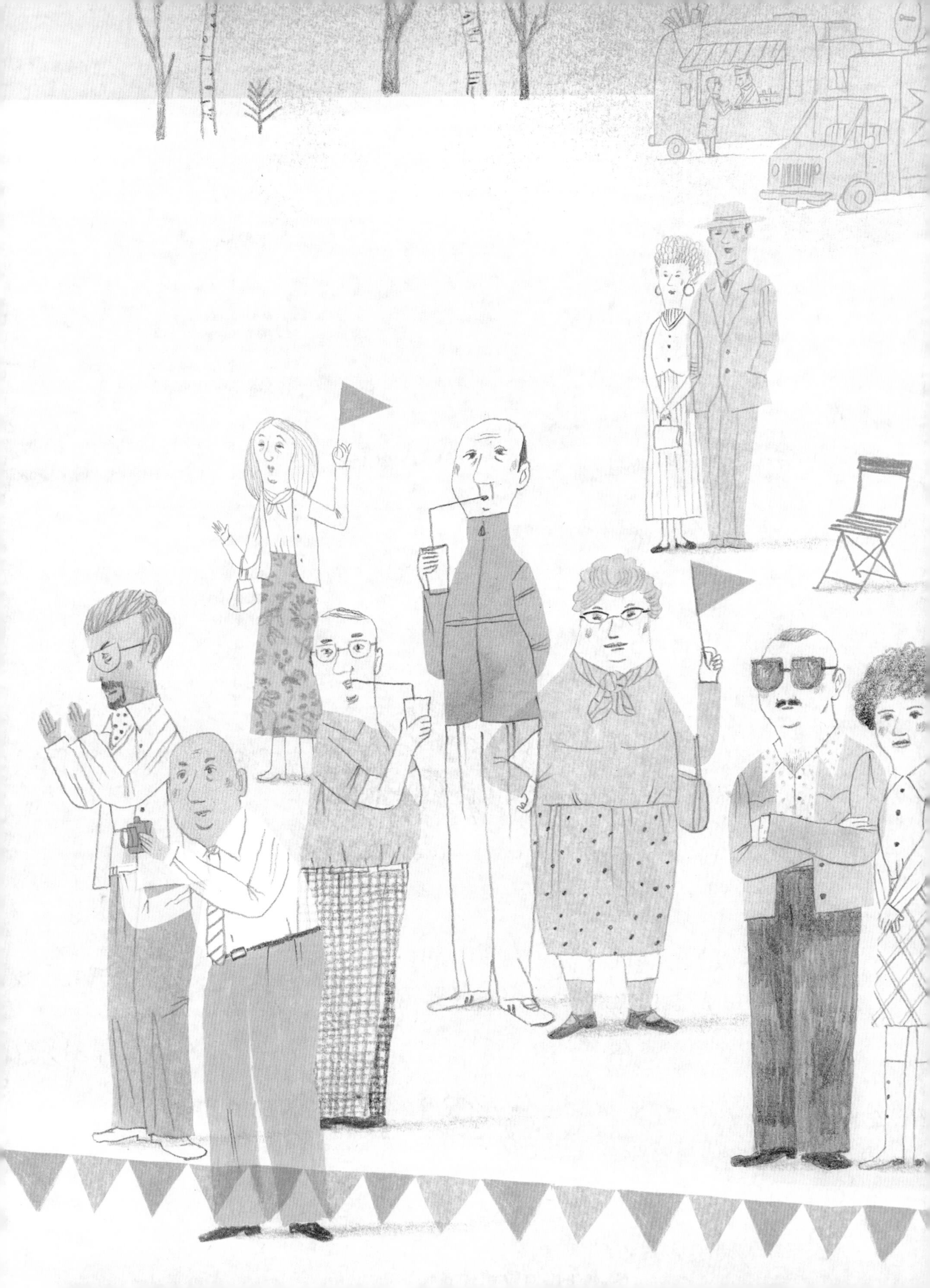

But there are some things you don't forget.

First there was
the noise of the engine that came up from
underneath my body
and made an unbelievable racket,
with a heat that rose up
into my throat.

And not long after that, the sea.
The sea that transformed right before my eyes
into a huge patch of blue —
a blue that would make
all the other blues of the world jealous.

Then the noise of my heart
which, after all,
had just had the shock of its life.

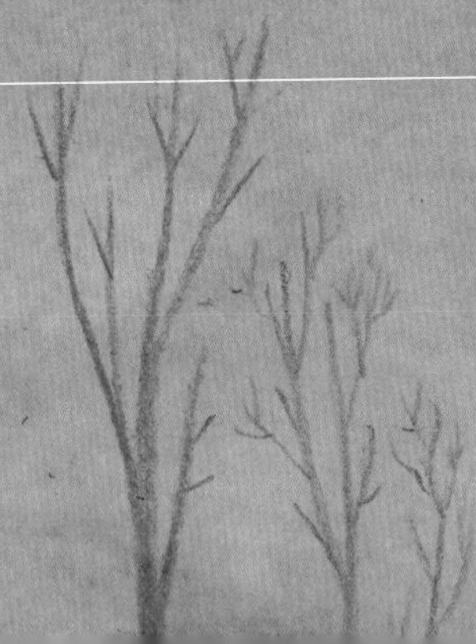

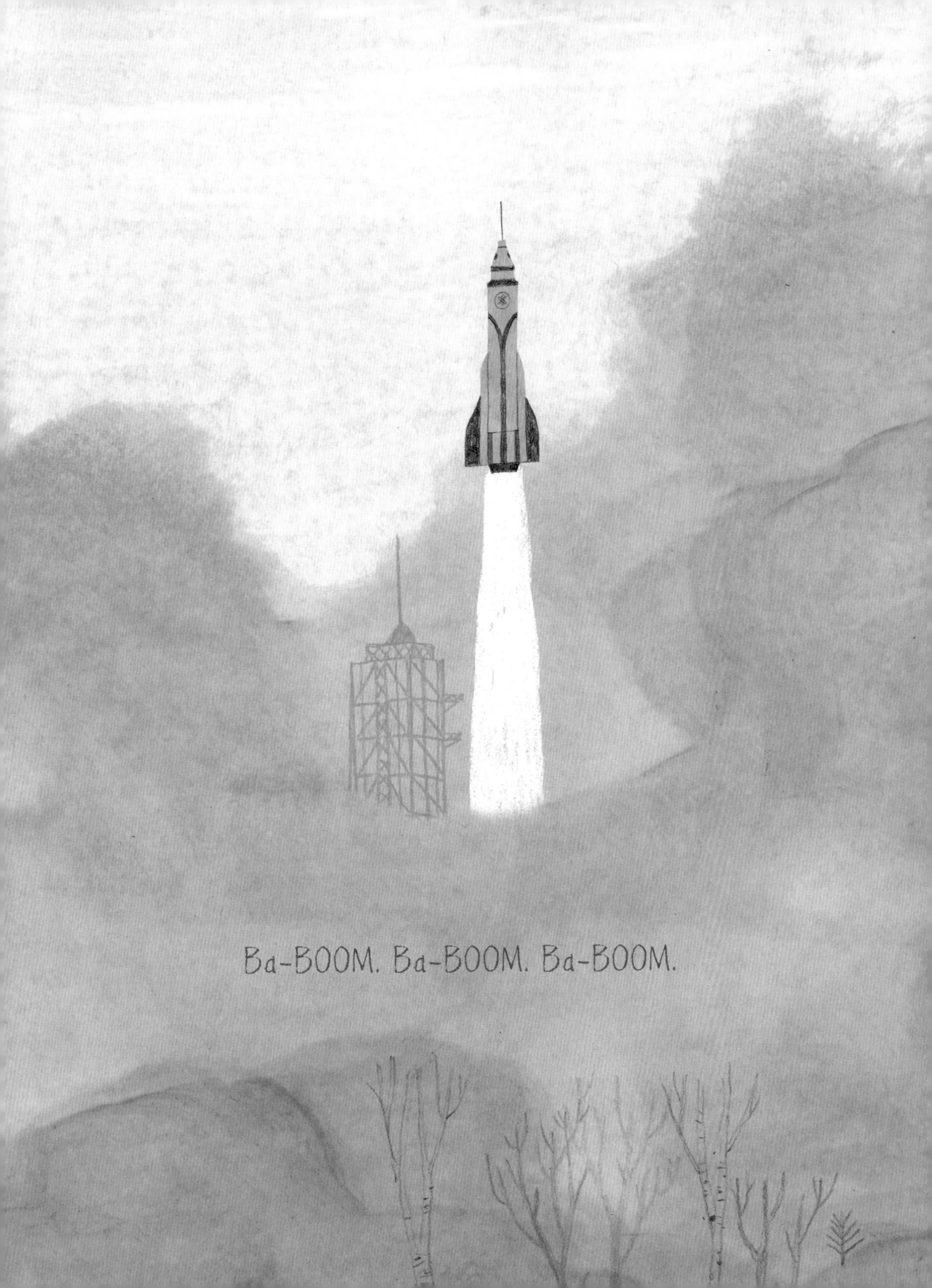

Ba-BOOM. Ba-BOOM. Ba-BOOM.

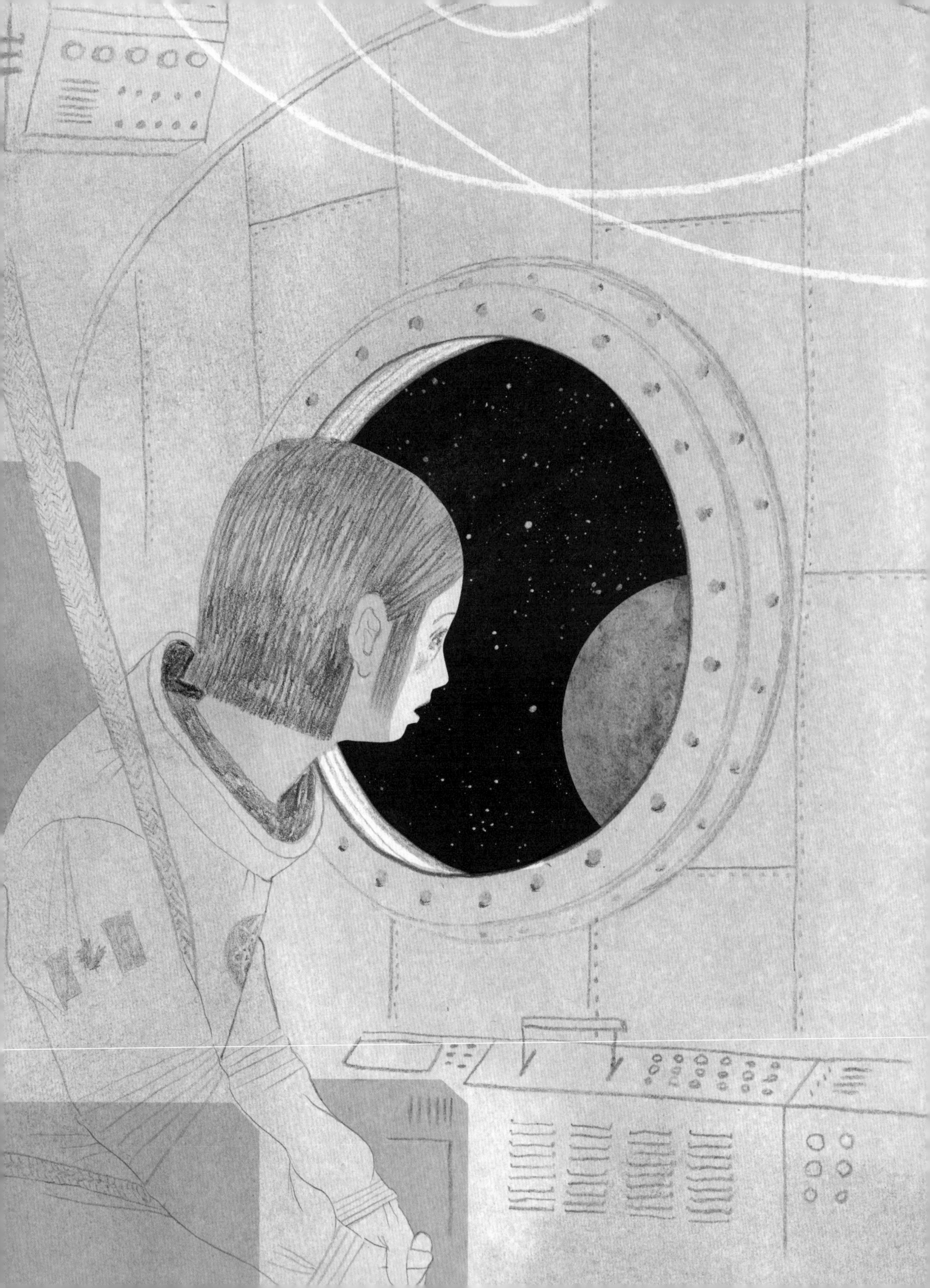

I say this not to make you envious
(that would be very rude),
but because it's true.
It is so beautiful up there,
it makes you want to cry.

That feeling of being so far away from everything,
even your cat ...

But since all good things come to an end
(Grandfather's the one who says this and you can bet
he knows what he's talking about),
it was like it always is after big fireworks and big
celebrations.
There was ...

an emptiness.

I thought it was one of those black holes that exist in space
and that suck everything in,
even well-trained astronauts
(who all know that it's best to stay away from black holes).

But it wasn't a black hole, of course, because otherwise
I wouldn't be here to tell you about it.

We can't know or understand everything in life,
and for once I have to confess that
I'm not sure I can tell you
what got into me that I suddenly felt so ...
empty.

I don't know what got into my eyes, either,
that made them shut
(no matter how much I tried to keep them open)
just when I was about to reach
the moon.

It's true that so close to the stars —
the shooting stars, but also the dead ones that are still holding
on (each one more beautiful than the last),
I quickly began to feel a bit faint.

It's also true that without warning,
like it had always been there just waiting for this moment,
the silence came in and sat down very close to me.
And to see it there, not moving,
would have freaked anyone out.

(It was the kind of silence
where you could hear a pin drop.)

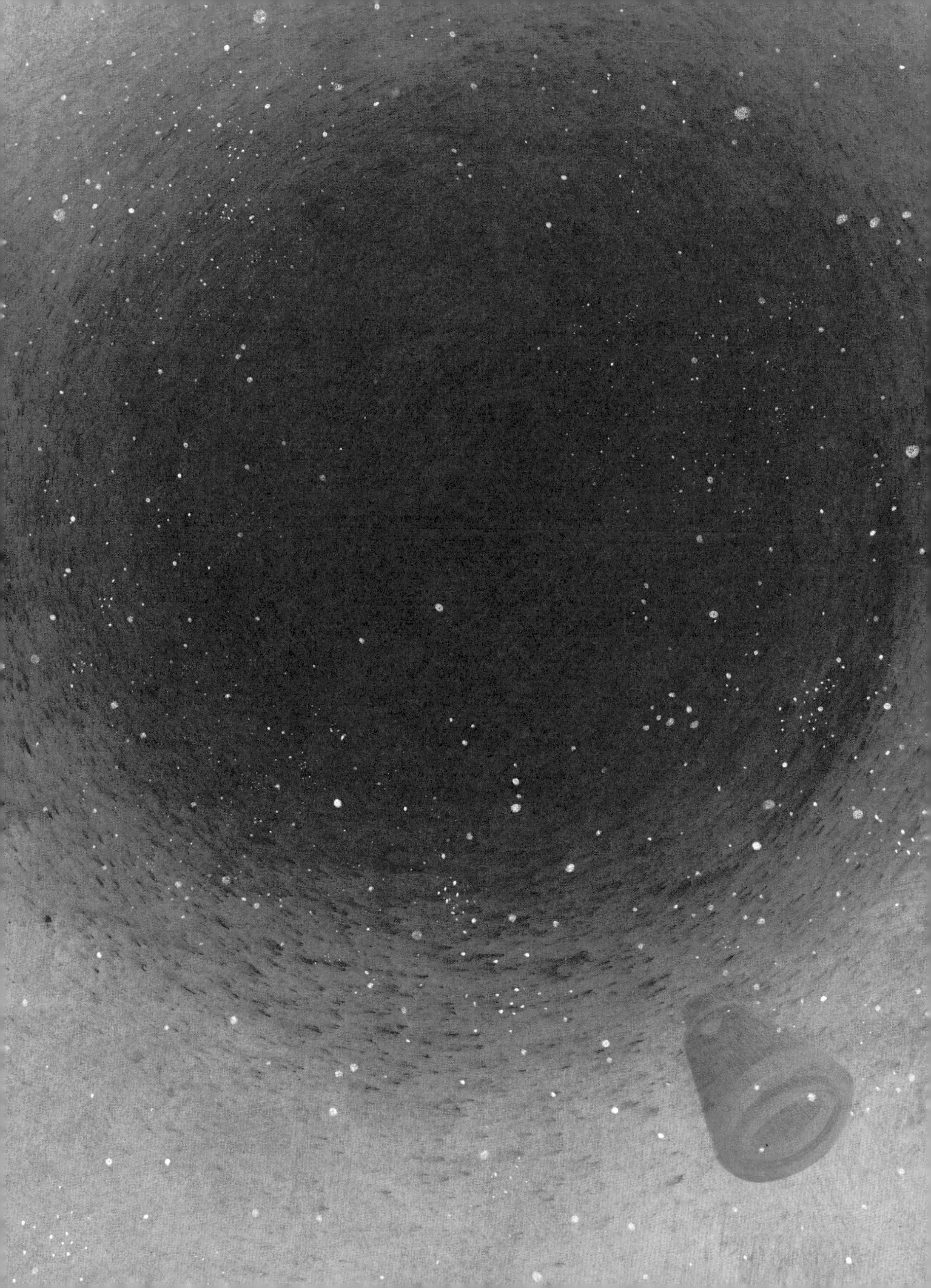

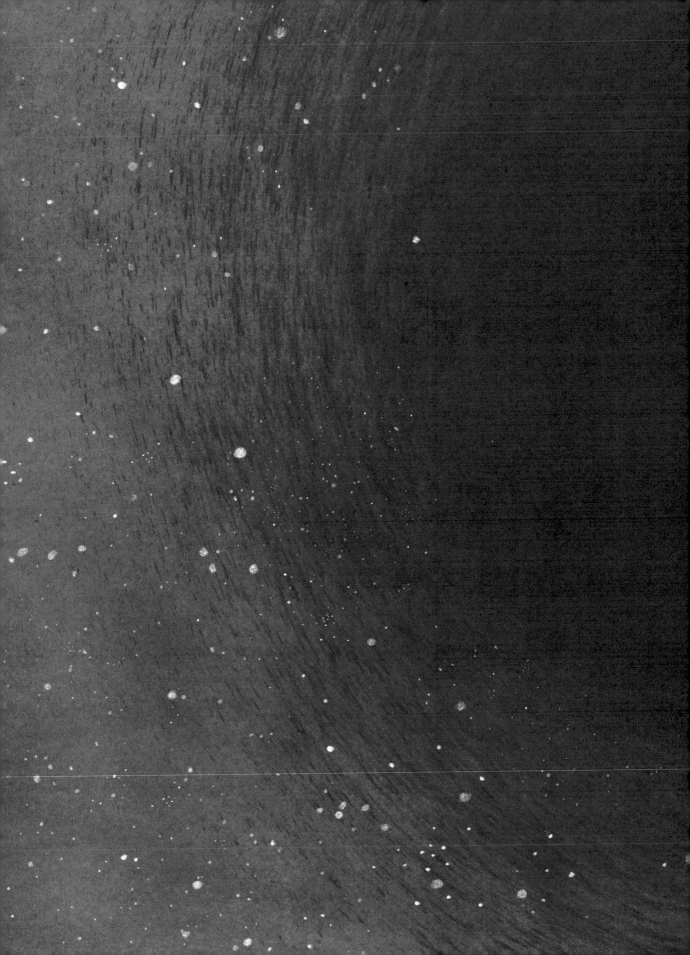

Real astronauts are prepared for this kind of thing.

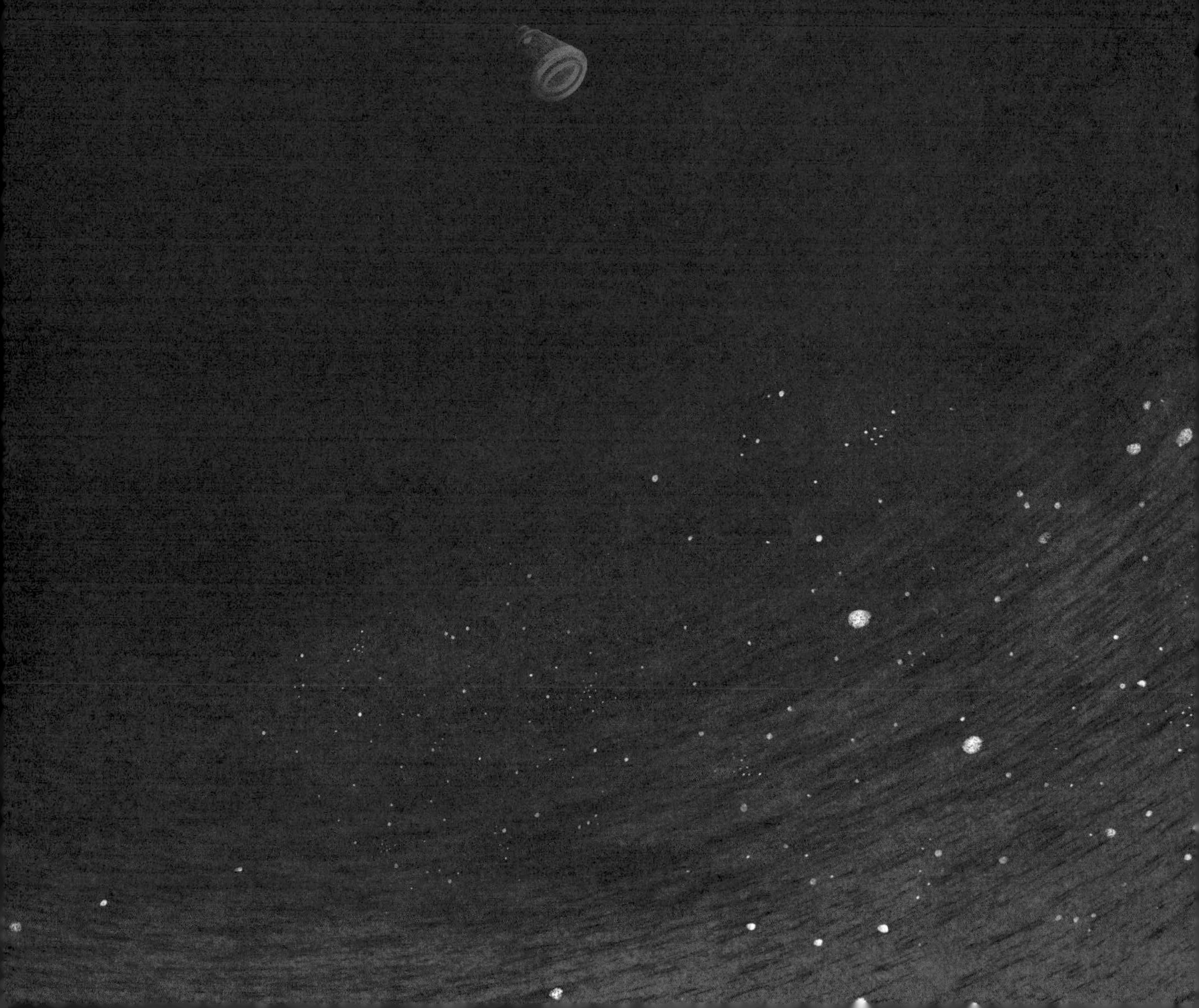

But of course it would have taken too long
to tell the people in line
about this.

Too long and
it would have made it sound like a lot less fun.

That's probably why they called it
the Who Will Go to the Moon Contest.

And not, for example,
the Who Will or Won't Like the Silence and the Stars
That Aren't Dead or That Might Be Dead but That Keep
Hanging in There Contest.

It's a minor detail.
A trivial matter.
But when you really think about it,
it's the details and trivia
that make up pretty much
everything.

As I was saying, I was on the verge of reaching the moon,
when my eyelids just shut tight over my eyes, plunging
them into darkness,
and I realized at that point that maybe the best thing to
do would be just
to sit back and think about things.

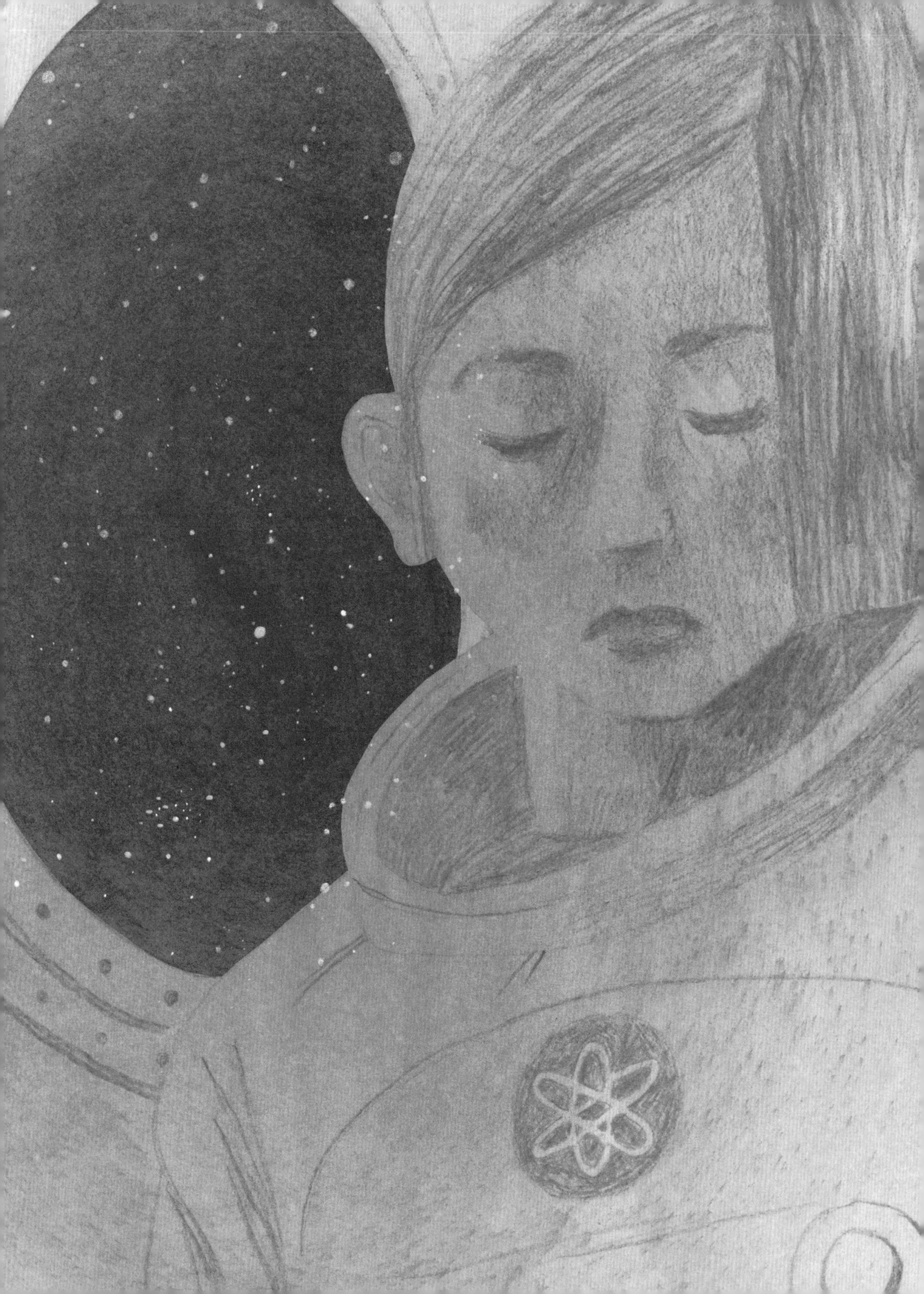

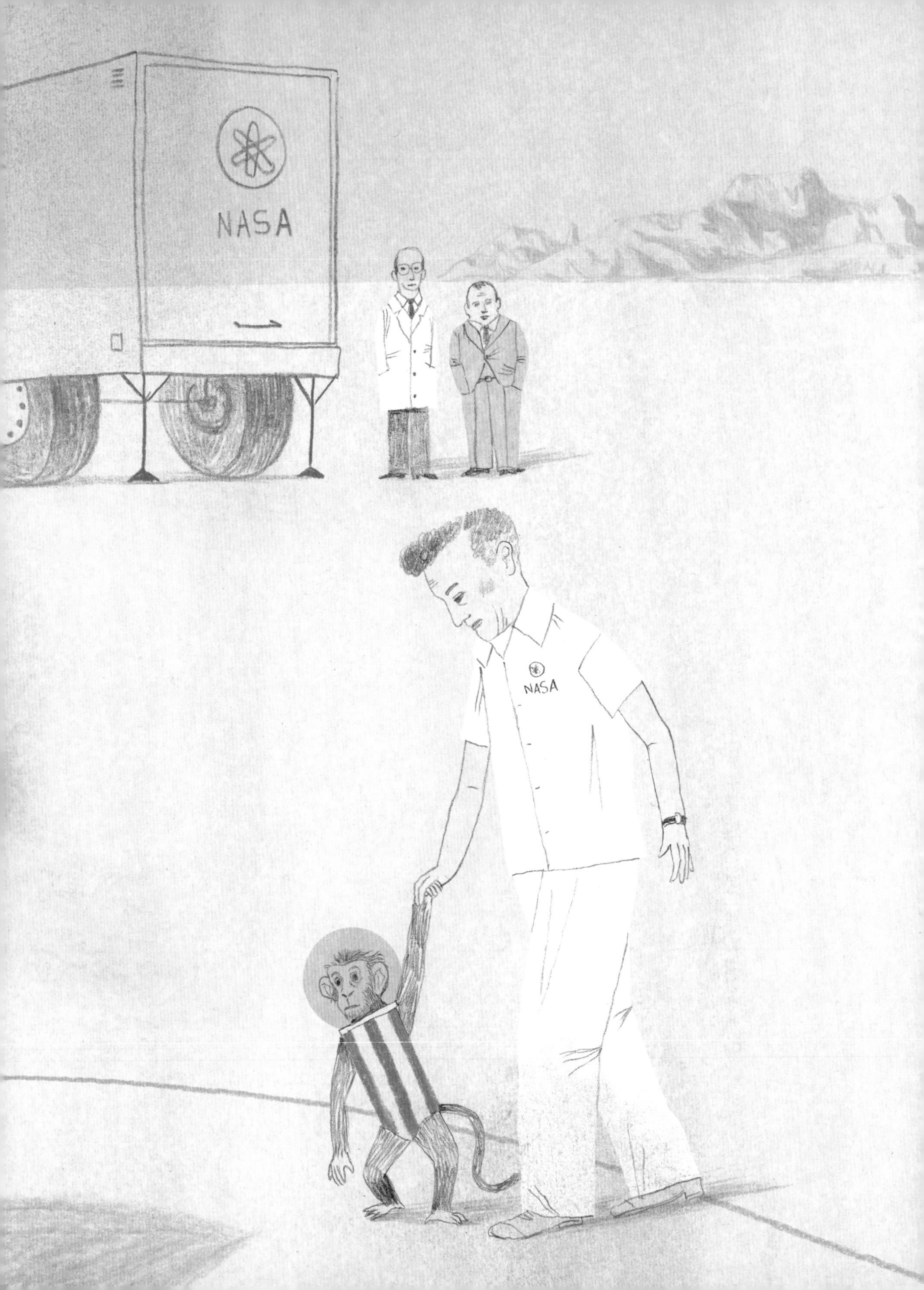
NASA
NASA

So I started to think about
the monkey, Albert,
who was sent into space
Friday, June 11, 1948.

That was way before Yuri Gagarin.

The guys at NASA were afraid to go themselves,
so they sent him instead.

Someone had to go first.

What's on the mind
of a monkey
dressed in an astronaut suit?

NASA

Maybe at the moment of liftoff,
Albert fought his fear
by thinking about what his friends would say about him
when he got back.

Albert, the space pioneer.
Albert, the one who knows how to fly.
Albert, a monkey like no other.

But maybe he was also wondering
whether it wouldn't have been good just to grow old
as a boring monkey.

Still, the NASA guys found that their project
worked out fantastically,
and they orchestrated five other launches in the "Albert"
series between 1948 and 1951.

With monkeys all named Albert.

But Albert didn't know
about all that.

Oxygen is quite scarce up there.

Maybe it was all this thinking about monkeys in space.

Or maybe it was that my body
was lost inside
my too-big astronaut suit.

Or maybe the signs the crowd was waving
were too sparkly
around the edges.

Or maybe the flashbulbs
were too bright
in my face.

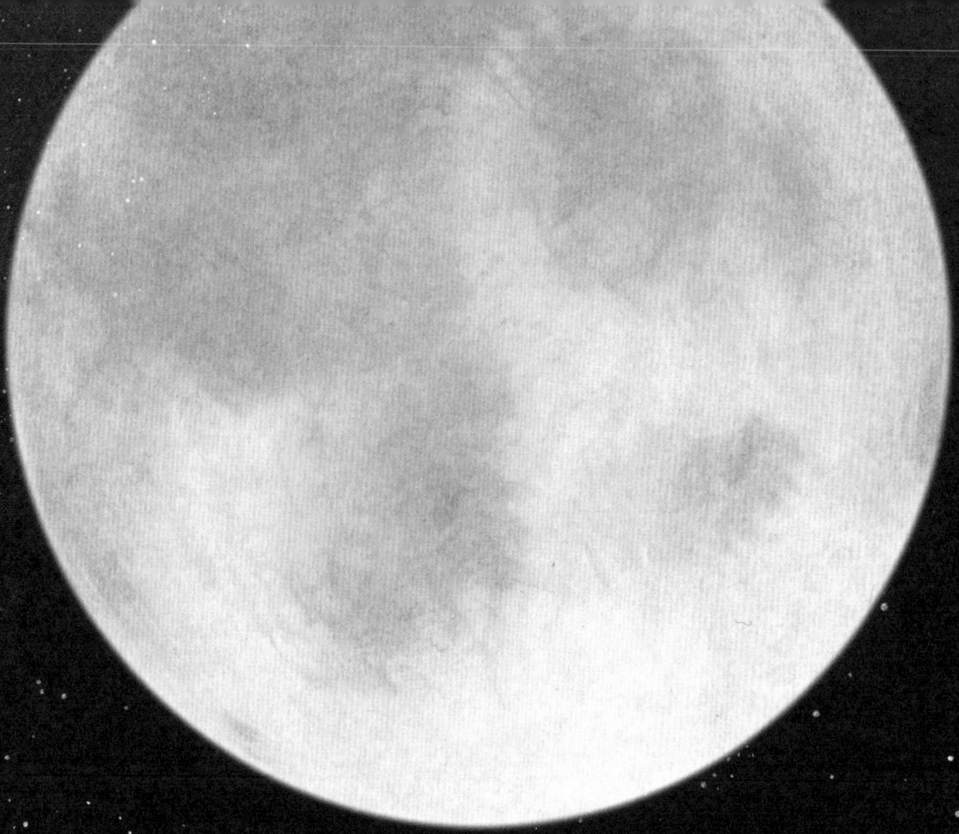

Or maybe it was just
that the moon
isn't for everyone.

But that morning,

I would have liked Grandfather to come and pick me up
in his gray Chrysler shaped like a box of soap.

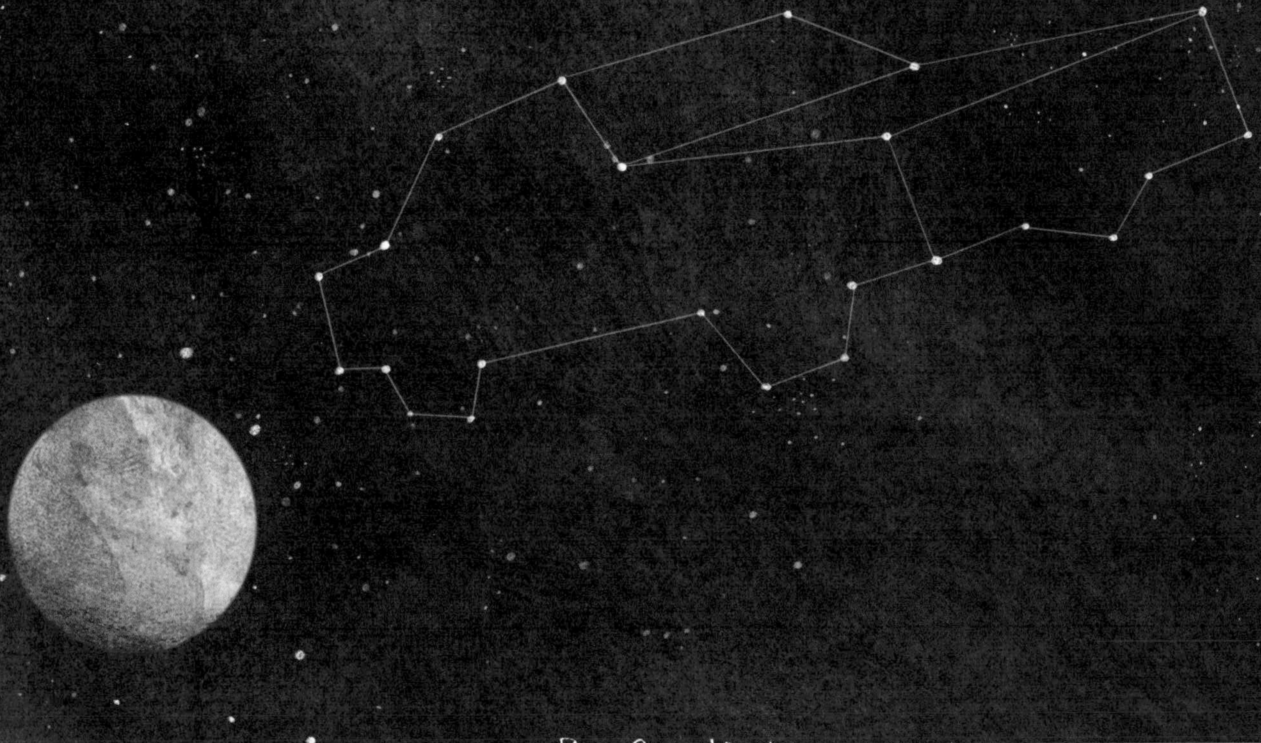

But Grandfather wasn't there.

How do you know
when you've disappointed
a man of few words?

Maybe I lied to Grandfather
when I told him that everything would be the same
when I got back.

And when I told him
that you had to get a degree
to be an astronaut.

Grandfather wouldn't have believed me
if I told him that it was enough
— the way it was for Albert —
just to draw the winning number.

Number 6506

That morning I thought that
if Albert the monkey had known that
five other Alberts
identical to him
would be sent into space

(as well as a Russian dog, a cat and eleven mice)

and that the real pioneer of outer space
would never be him
but Yuri Gagarin,

a cosmonaut
worthy of the name,
to human eyes,

maybe he would have said to himself,

What's the point?

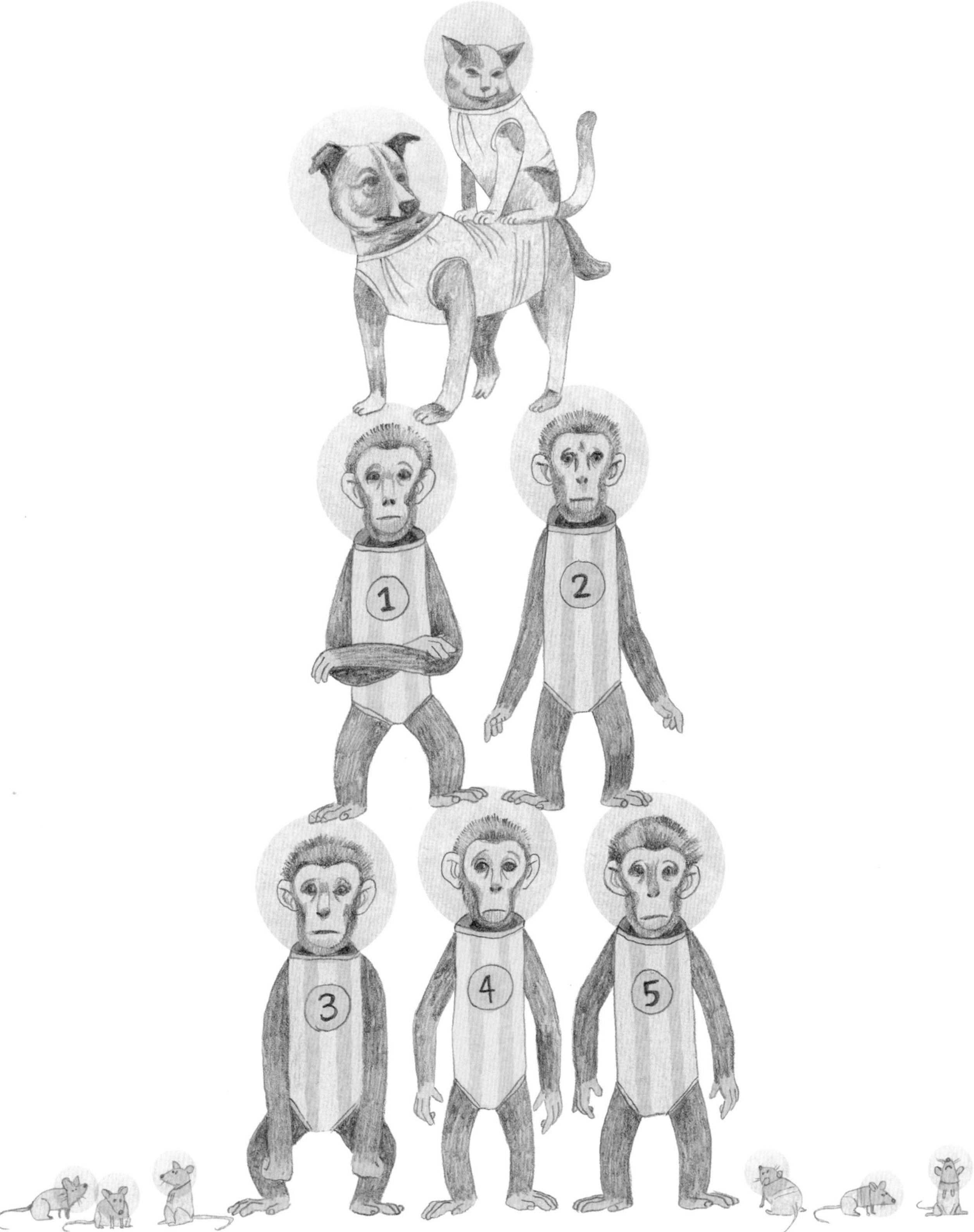
1
2
3
4
5

I figured he might even have ejected himself from the rocket.

Who knows?

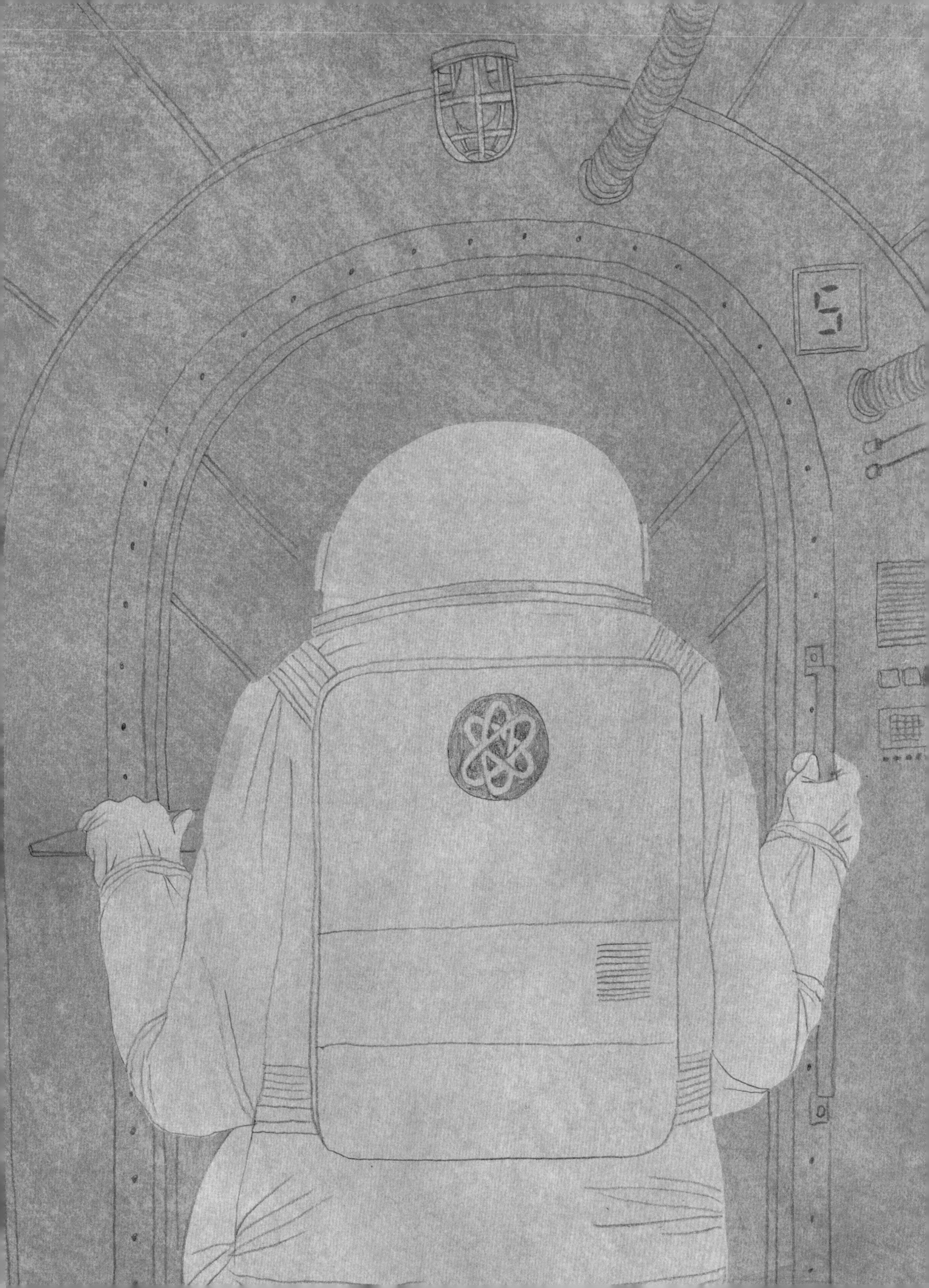
5

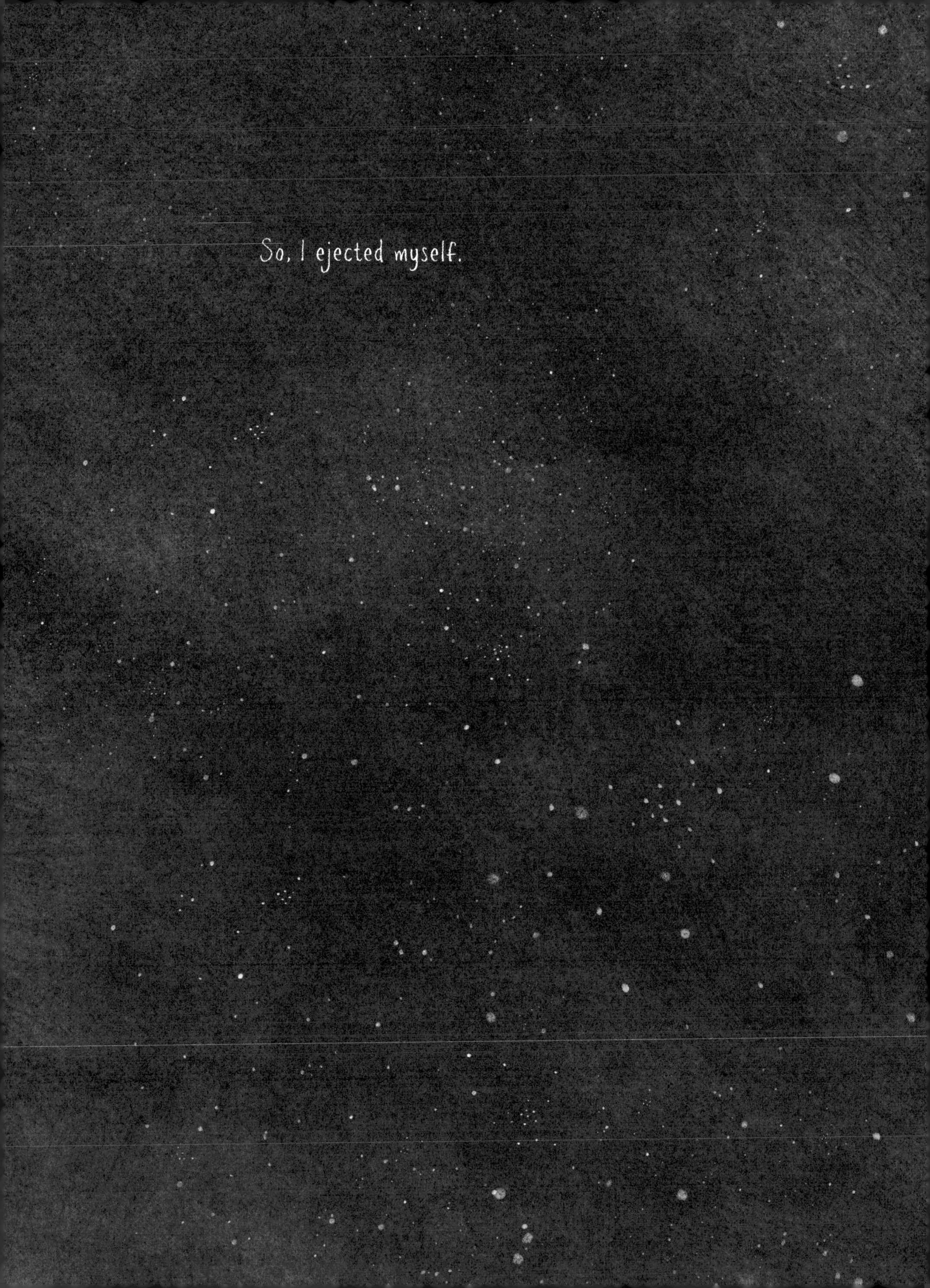

So, I ejected myself.

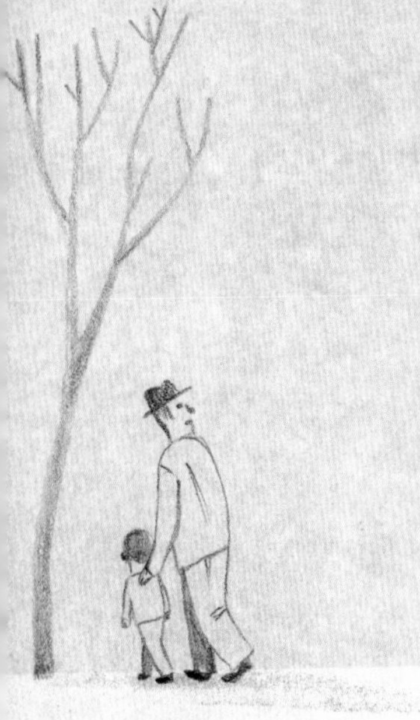

Many looked up in horror,
and the crowd scattered
as quickly as it had gathered,

when they realized that no one
would be going to the moon
that morning

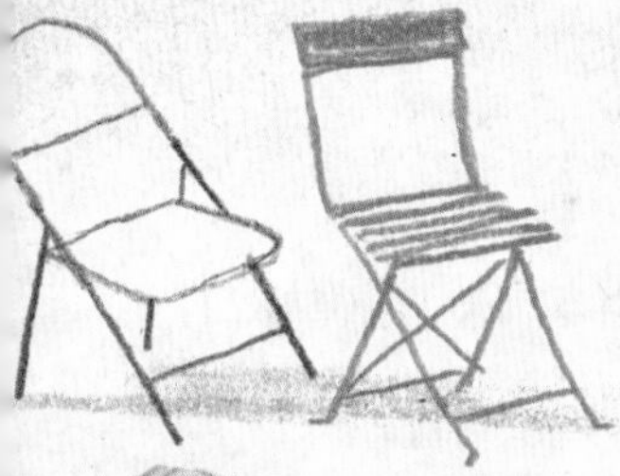

and that the show
was over.

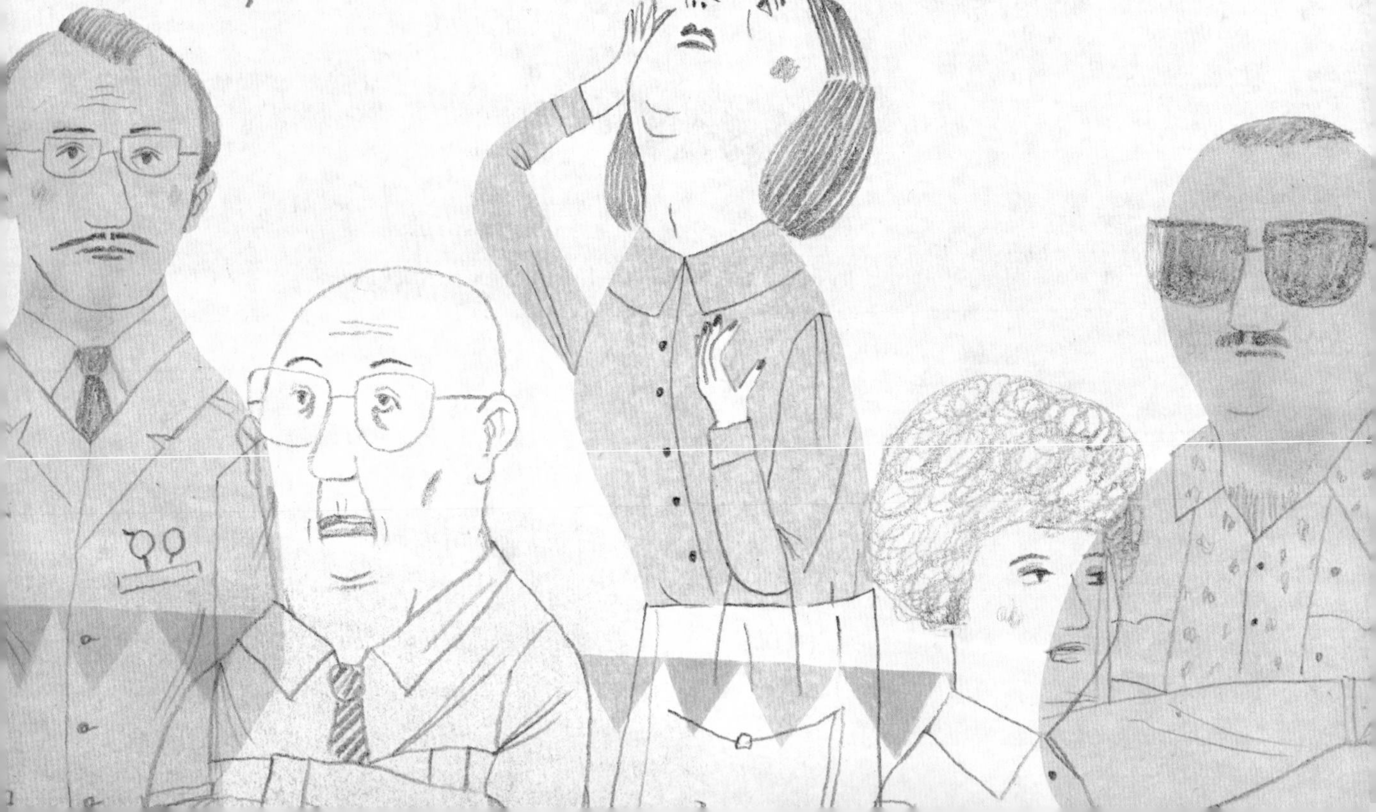

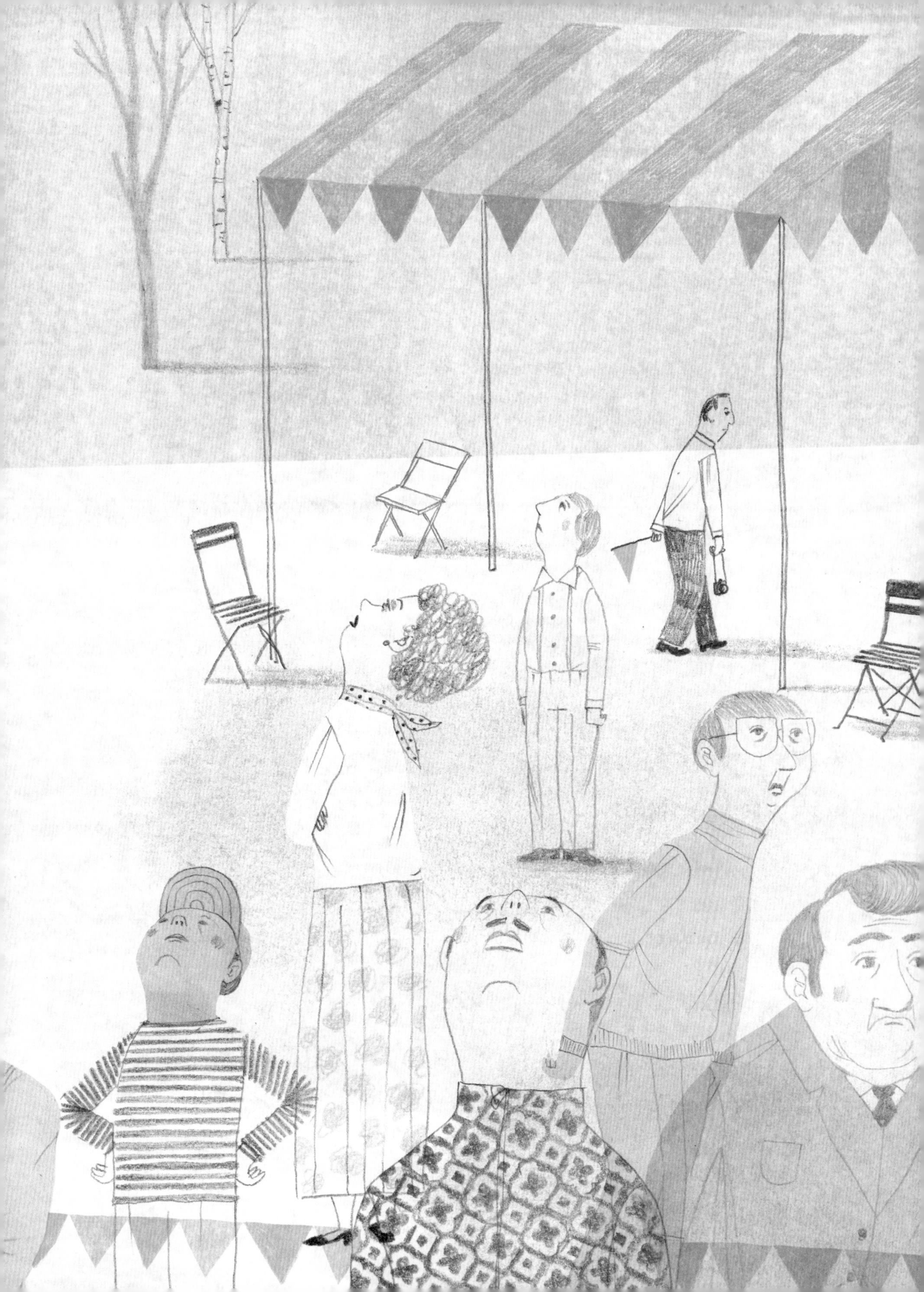

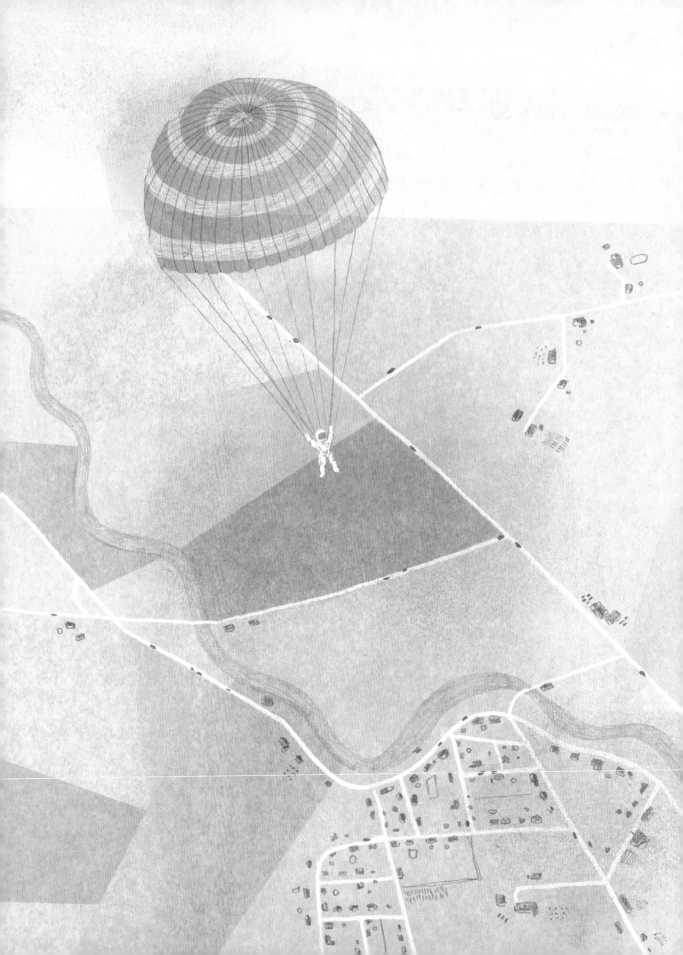

Of course I was ashamed
of taking someone else's spot.
Someone who would do anything
to see the moon.

Of course I was ashamed of my body,
which was tossed
from left to right,
wherever the wind took it.

And of course I was ashamed
that I would never
get a degree
to be an astronaut.

And what's more,
I would never see the moon.

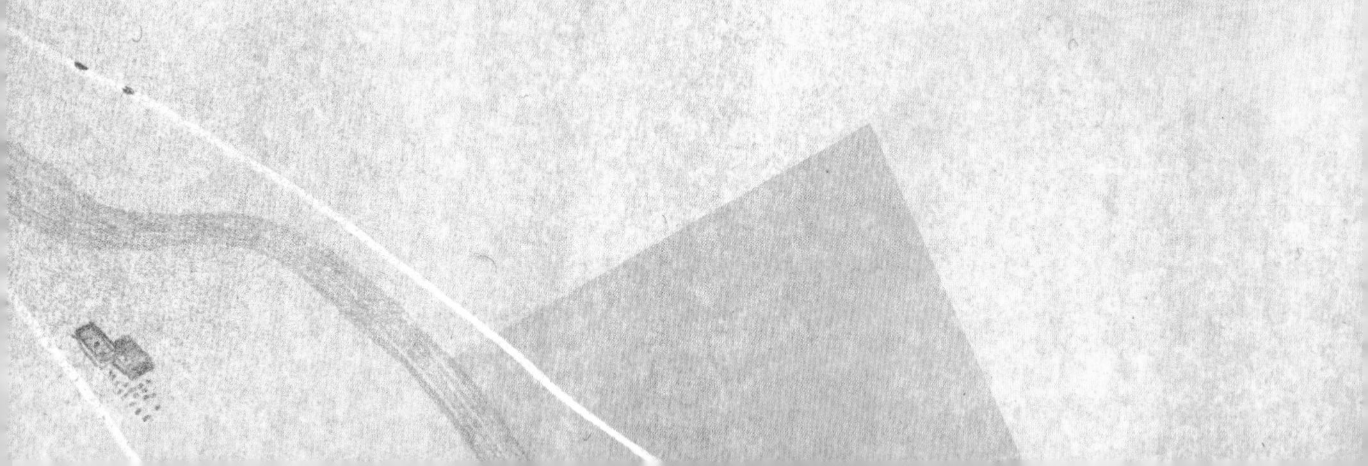

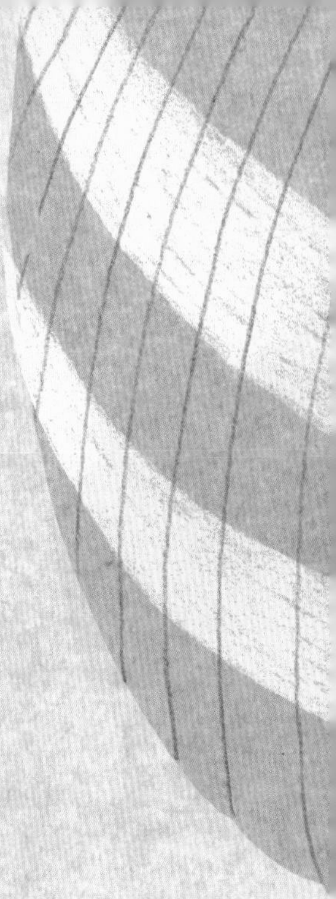

So I started to imagine
letting go of the lines of my parachute,

thinking maybe
that would be the best thing to do
when someone wanted to give you the moon

and you didn't take it.

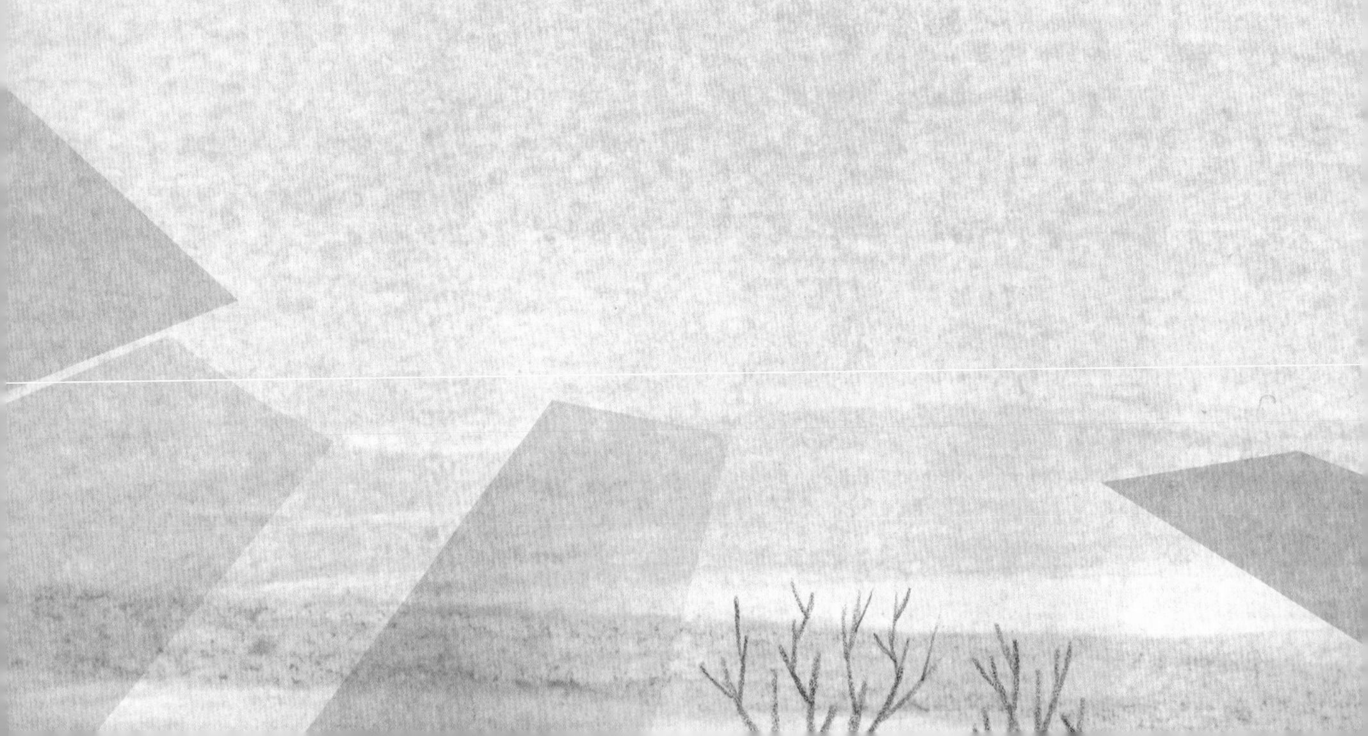

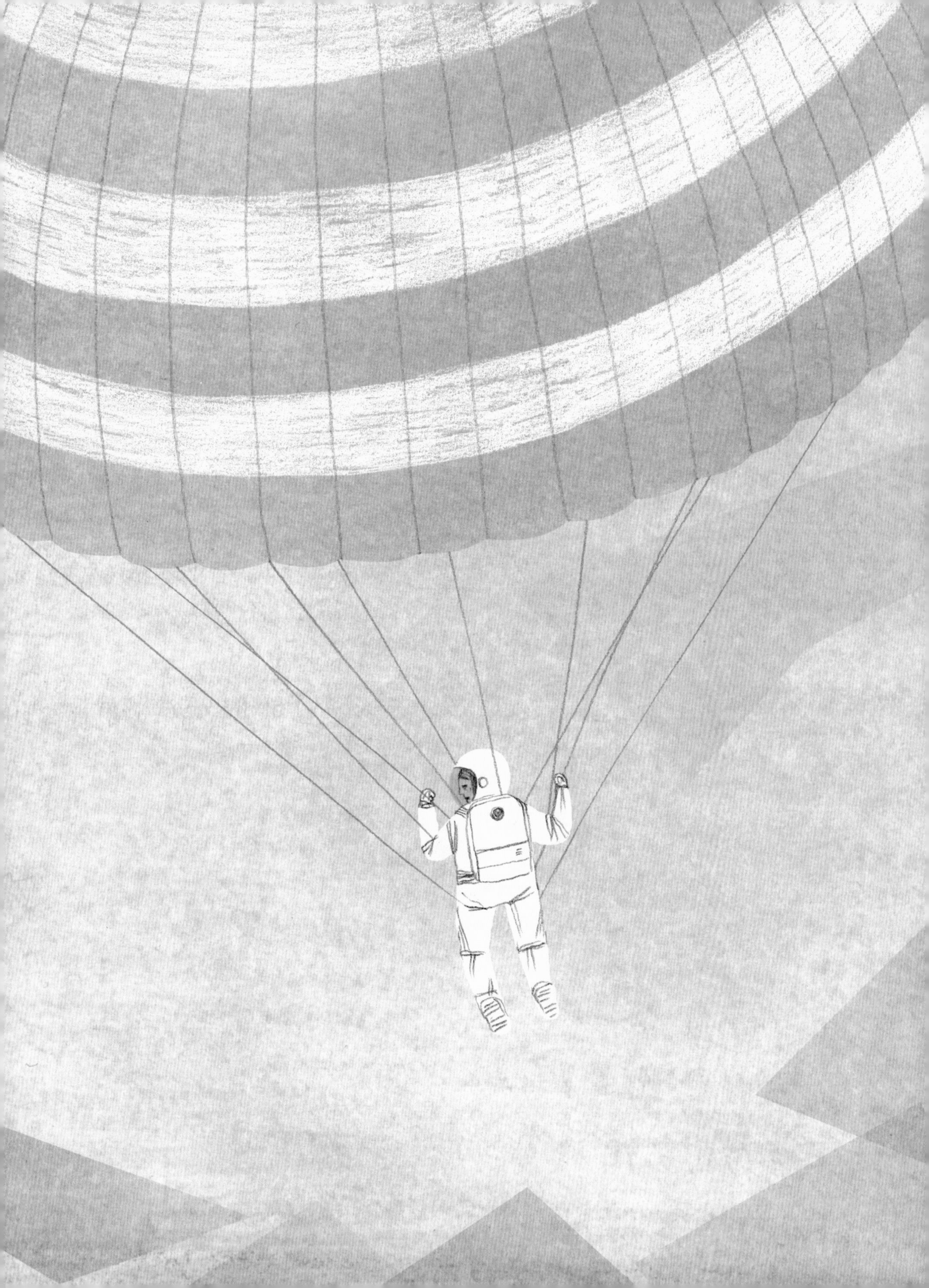

Hard to say whether it was destiny
or chance
(you have to know, first of all, which
you believe in),

but at exactly that moment,
a few dozen meters
beneath my feet,

I noticed a man

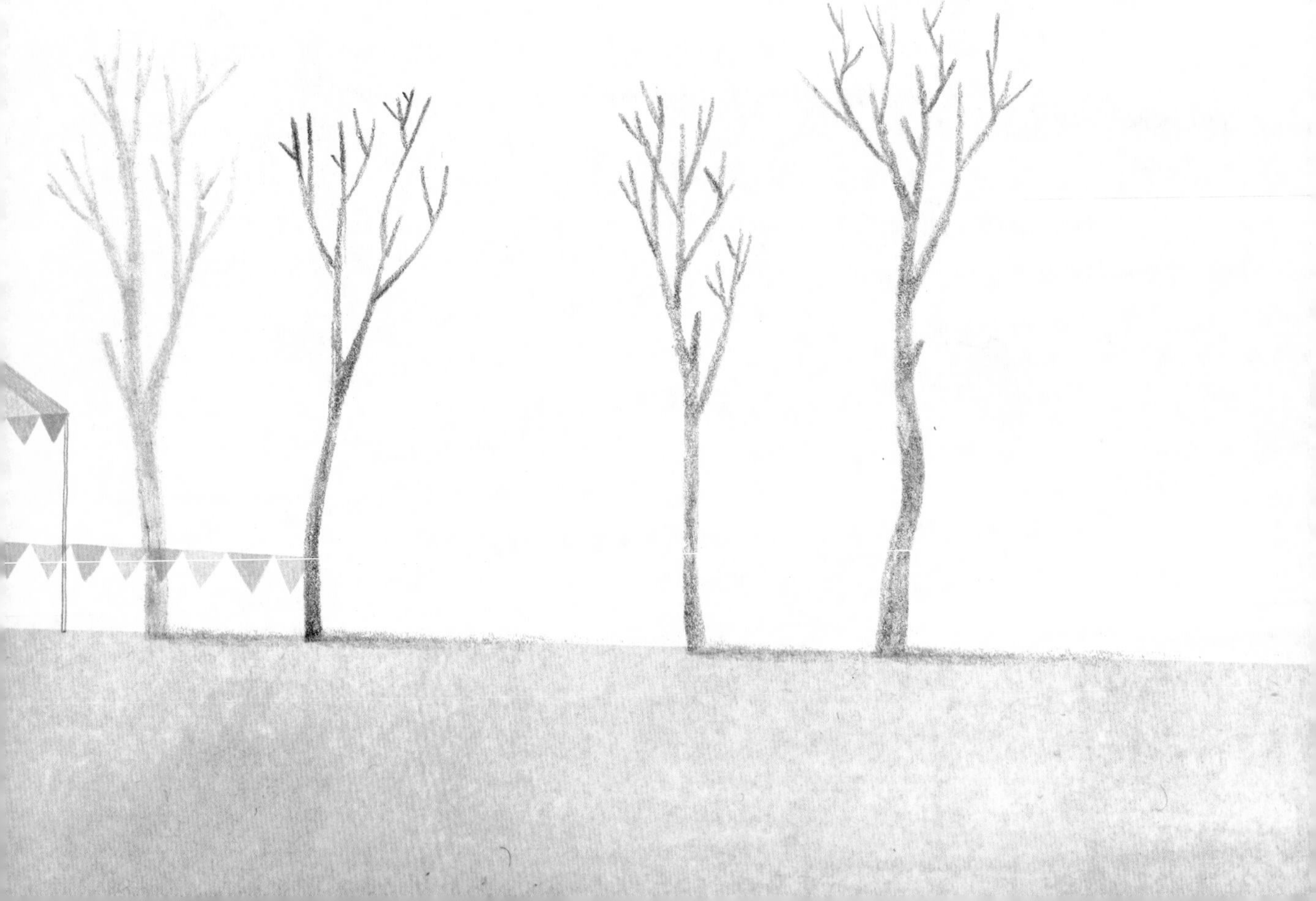

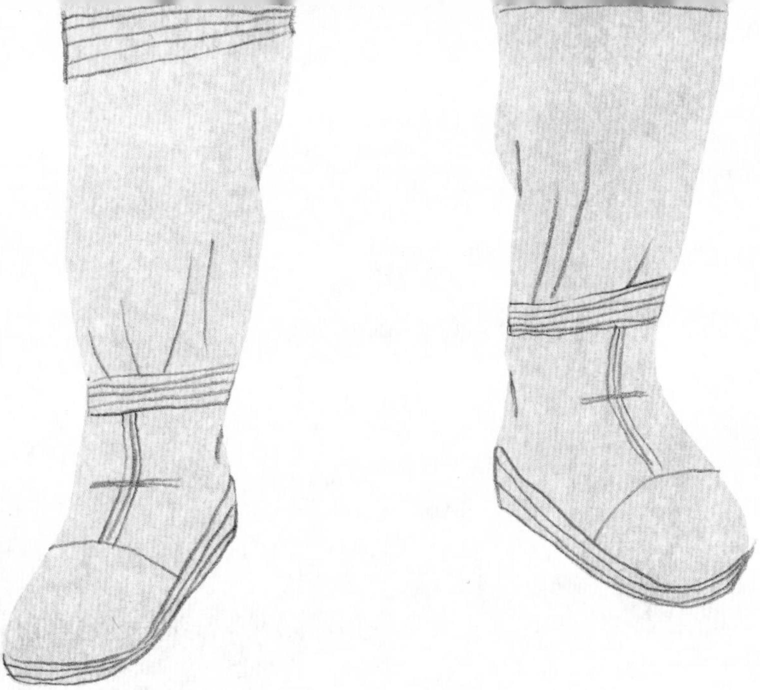

sitting in a gray Chrysler
shaped like a box of soap.

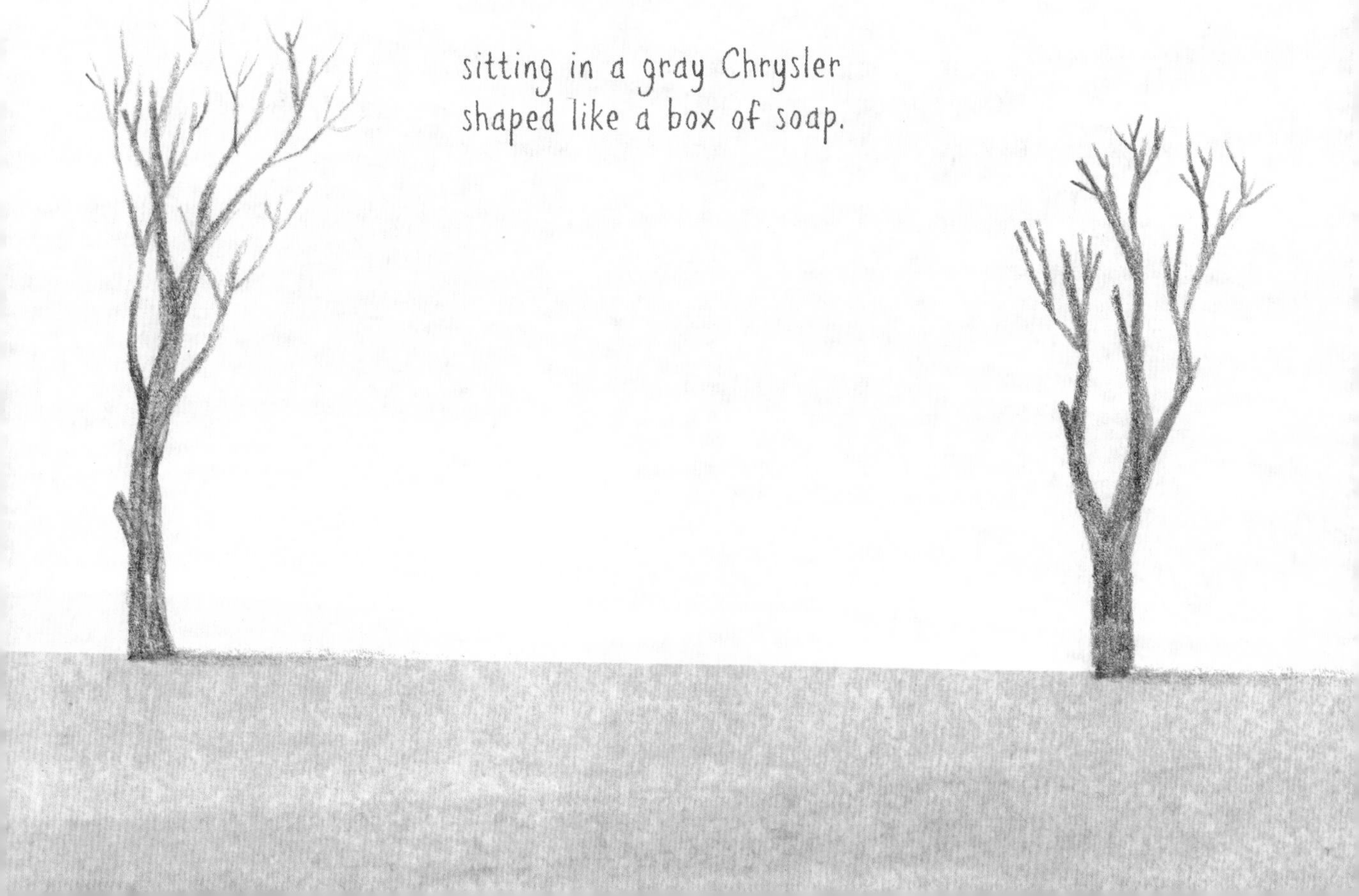

So while everyone was arguing
over whether the story was true or not
about the parachute being
open or closed

(they couldn't tell anymore),

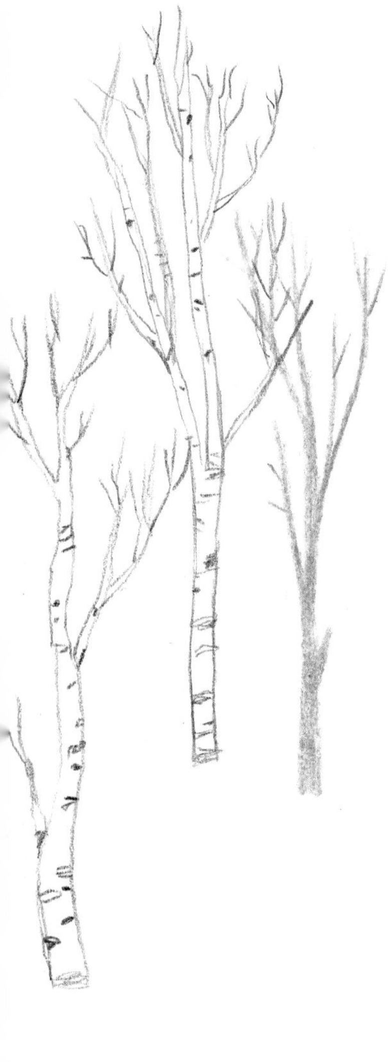

there he was,
off to the side,
fast asleep.

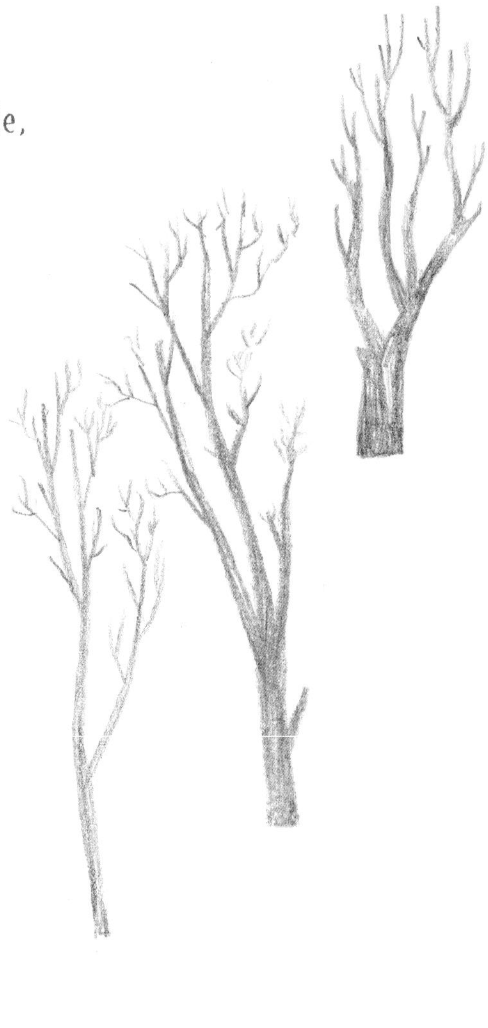

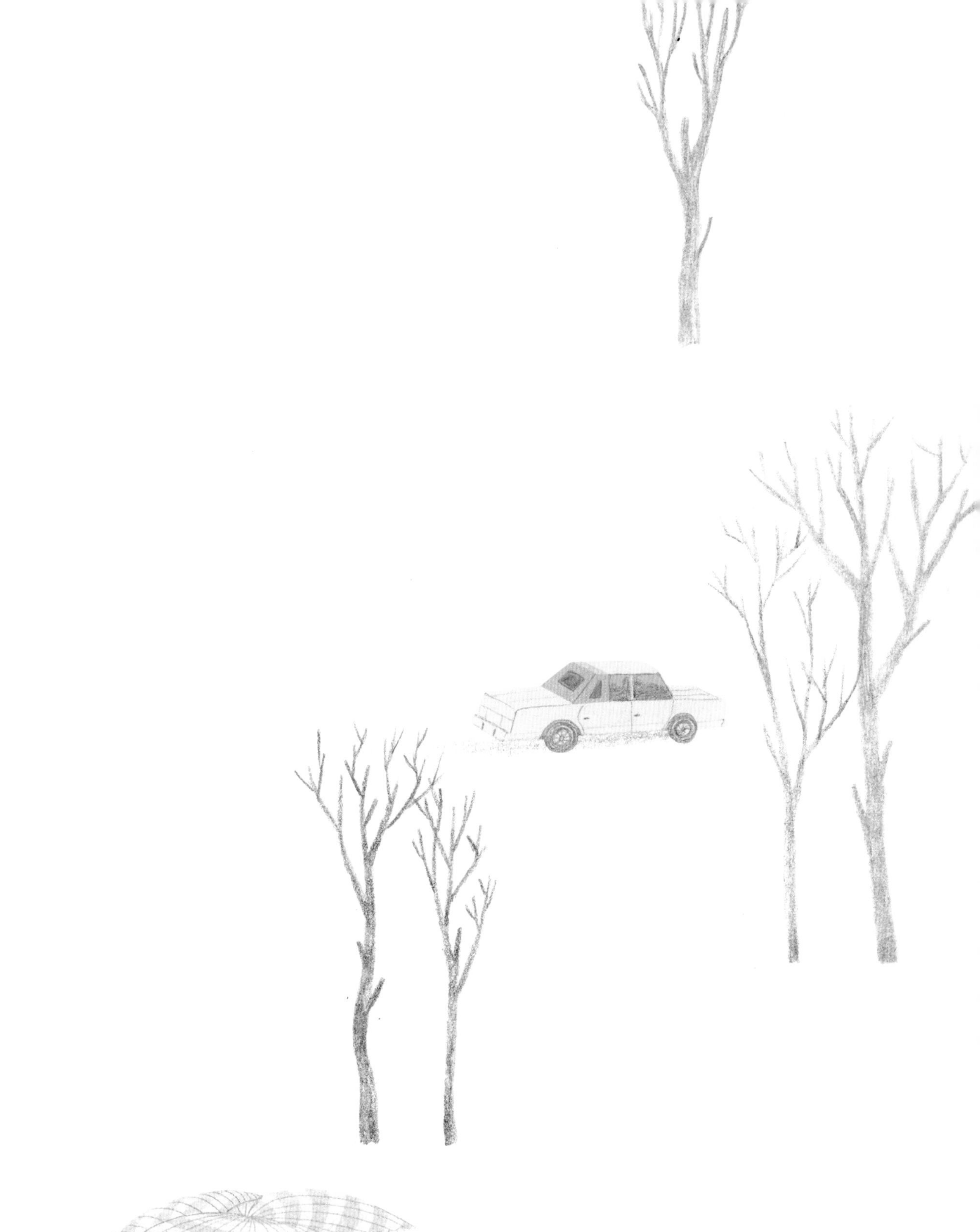

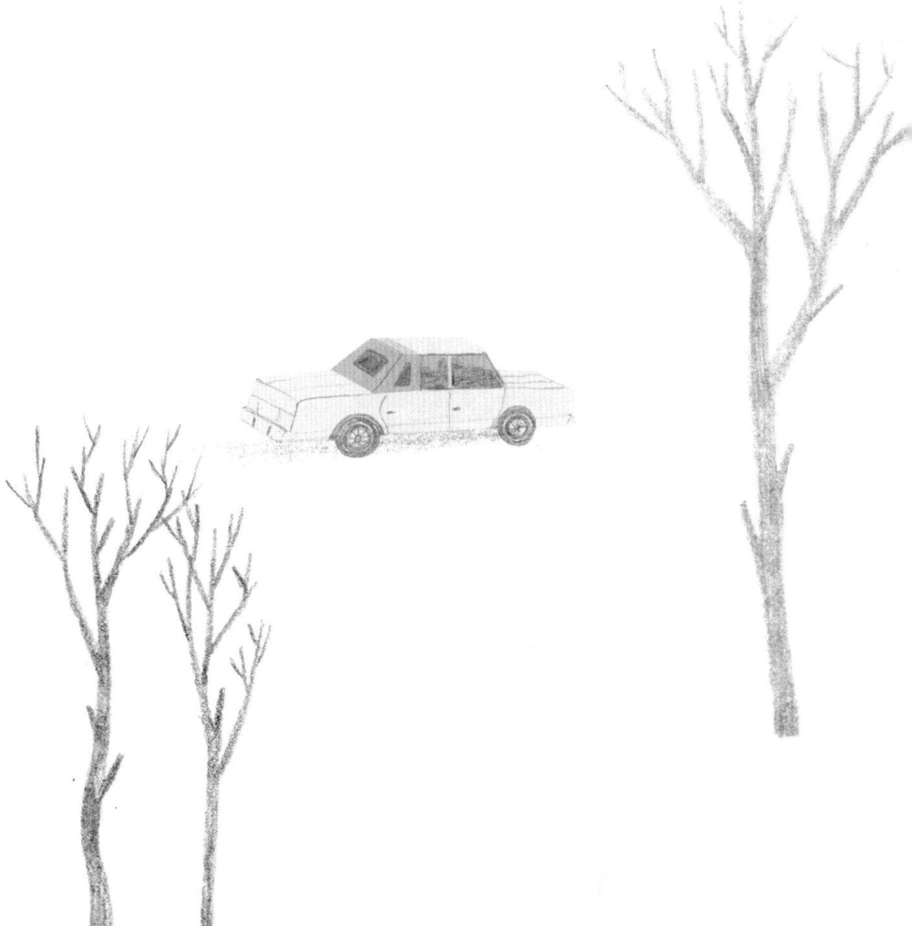

Stéphanie Lapointe is a singer and actress who has produced three solo albums and is involved in various television, theater and film productions. She has co-directed several documentaries abroad for Radio Canada International and Care Canada. She is also the author of the young adult novel *Victoria*. Stéphanie lives in Montreal.

Rogé is an illustrator, painter and writer with more than twenty children's books to his credit, including *Haiti, My Country: Poems by Haitian School Children*, which was named a New York Times Best Illustrated Children's Book. He has won two Governor General's Literary Awards, most recently for the illustrations in this book. Rogé lives in Montreal.

Shelley Tanaka is an award-winning author, translator and editor who has written and translated more than thirty books for children and young adults. She teaches at Vermont College of Fine Arts, in the MFA Program in Writing for Children and Young Adults. She lives in Kingston, Ontario.